Forever is Now

Elin Annalise

First published in November 2024 by Ineja Press

Cover Design by Sarah Anderson Designs
Interior Formatting by Sarah Anderson Designs
Editing by Madelaine Couch

Paperback ISBN: 978-1-912369-48-5
eBook ISBN: 978-1-912369-47-8

Elin Annalise

Forever is Now

INEJA PRESS

INTRODUCTION

Summer

Everyone thinks they know our story. But no one knows the truth.

Not even Ruari knows the truth.

Only I know the truth—my truth—and that really gets to me sometimes, makes me want to cry and wail, curl up into a ball and just disappear. Because I've spent these last six months trying to get the world to believe me more than ever. Begging them to.

And they don't want to.

My name is Summer Eloise Taylor-Braddon. I'm twenty-nine years old, but I expect you already know that. You think you know me. You've seen me in the news. Me and Ruari Braddon, or the new name he goes by. Robert Haydon. You know what happened. How me and Ruari were childhood sweethearts, how we got married, and then how he went missing on our honeymoon.

You'll know the next bit, too. How the years passed with no news on my Ruari. How I had no idea if he was even alive. How the media tried to drag my name through the mud. How I wrote our love story, instead of living it. Got on the *Sunday Times* bestseller list, then the *New York Times* and *USA Today* lists, too. Bled my grief and anguish into the page.

And how, six years after he disappeared, he was found. Living a new life. Retrograde amnesia, doctors said.

And then I expect you think you know what I did and who died—because the press *really* loves talking about that. Making me out to be the murderer. The jilted bride driven to revenge. Some said I was insane. Some said I was a psychopath.

But, as I'm sure you know, the thing about journalists is that they twist things. They want clickbait, snappy headlines, and they don't care about the truth.

I know that better than anyone. But I care about the truth.

I tried to write a memoir. In fact, I did. Three hundred pages of rawness bled me dry.

I had it attached to my email, ready to send to my agent, but I couldn't press send.

Because I knew. People would still say I was lying.

I needed something different.

Something to counter Adelaide James's lies.

And the way to do that? Well, you'll see what I've done. What we've done.

Mum was not happy when I told her about this project. In fact, she's still not happy now. But she and I? Soon, we will no longer exist.

What follows is everything that Adelaide and I have come up with for this final exposé: transcripts, interviews, articles—every prominent voice in the conversation.

We thought it might be a podcast, and then we thought we'd make it into a TV drama show. My sister's got some contacts with directors and whatnot. She is just waiting for me to give the go ahead. But, really, I don't know what I want this to be.

A TV drama would cut parts because they'd want to make it more exciting.

A podcast would likely turn this into a True Crime thing, when really it's not.

It's a love story. It's raw, it's full of pain, but it's reality. My reality.

And so, for now, it's just this. These are the original transcripts, our actual conversations, nothing re-

recorded or taken out of the conversation, because these are our words in their truest forms. Sometimes, it's just me talking for what seems like hours at a time.

We got others involved, because stories never exist in isolation, in vacuums. And, well, I don't want you to have to take just my word for it. Hear from my friends, my family, even the people I don't like.

Forever is Now is what I have called this collection of everything *me and Ruari,* because those were the last words he said to me when he was still Ruari. My Ruari.

I want you all to know my story, even those of you who don't want to believe me. I want to pin your eyelids open and make you see what really happened. And if you still think I deserve everything that's happened since Ruari came back, well, then so be it.

But at least you'll know the truth.

Day One
Sunday July 21st, 2024

Adelaide James: So, Ms. Taylor-Braddon, I must admit, I was *astonished* when your agent got in touch. In fact, I choked on my breakfast. Avocado and smoked salmon on toast. A fancy Japanese herbal tea. I'd spent ages making it, setting out on the plate just right, using the tea strainer that my mother always said was only for when we had guests—because I was celebrating that morning. Celebrating a recent article I'd written. I'd just won a major award, but your email eclipsed that. And you know what? I can't even *remember* tasting my breakfast. All I recall is the way my shoulders suddenly tingled, how tight my forehead felt, and how I just couldn't make my fingers move fast enough to type back. I was so sure you'd change your mind.

Summer Taylor-Braddon: I haven't.

Adelaide James: No, you haven't. Which makes me really curious as to what you can possibly say to change my mind—as I assume that is your goal?

Summer Taylor-Braddon: What is it they say? Fight fire with fire.

Adelaide James: And I am the fire. [*She laughs*] Well, I'm sure we'll get more into this all later on. I have a rough outline here of how you'd like to tackle the recording of all this… and I must say, it does seem pretty thorough. I believe one might even say that objectivity is your goal? And I can see we'll both, apparently, have time to put our own views across. So, shall we get started?

Summer Taylor-Braddon: Yes. [*She clears her throat*] Yes, I think we should.

Adelaide James: Then go right ahead, Ms. Taylor-Braddon. Change my mind.

[*Silence for five seconds*]

Summer Taylor-Braddon: I still find it astonishing that everyone wants to know about what happened. The whole world, watching our lives like we are a soap opera. Everyone feels invested, like they have a personal right to know what's happened.

Of course, you have put me through hell—but you know what hurts the most? The idea that I never loved Ruari, as if it's up to someone else, someone like you, to decide whether my love is real.

I have gone through hell.

So has he.

And Mia. All those reporters, outside the hotel, the hospital, my house, his father's house, Mia's house.

So, I'm going to talk about a particular moment first, before we'll then go through everything chronologically.

I was in the Grand Aux Hotel, just sitting in our room. The one me and Mum had booked, as soon as we'd had the news confirmed. That Ruari had been found.

I hadn't yet seen him, and I felt sick, so sick to my stomach. There was a tapestry on the wall. Medieval, suits of armor, horses, that sort of thing. Dark, rich colors, and the horses had weird faces, and all I could stare at were those faces.

Annmarie, one of the British consulates who'd been helping us navigate the whole mess, was in the room too. Sitting at the side, by the coffee-making facilities. I was on the edge of the bed. My mother too. She reached over to squeeze my knee. A reassuring touch. And we just waited. And waited. Ruari was... out there. Not just in the vague sense of the phrase, like I'd told myself so many times as I cried myself into a shallow state of sleeplessness where nightmares plagued me. But he was really and truly out there. Alive. Here.

There were fifteen minutes until he was due to arrive at the hotel. Fifteen minutes until I'd see the love of my life again, but all I could think about was that tapestry. The horses' eyes were too far forward on their faces. Like they'd never actually be able to see properly if anyone was sneaking up on them. Their field of vision was so limited.

Annmarie and my mother were talking. There were police stationed outside my hotel room, because of some of the threats we'd received, and I could hear their voices too. Most of them were speaking in French and I didn't really understand. Couldn't pick out more words than *remarquable!* and *il ne s'en souvient pas,* because those were the words that just kept being repeated, but it was reassuring to have them there. The police, that is. I felt… protected.

I'd received more death threats that morning. According to Annmarie, so had Ruari. She let that slip, when my mother was asking some questions. I can't even remember what.

You'd led people to think it was just all a publicity stunt. A sick game to get the world riled up. A sick game to boost my book sales.

Adelaide James: You—

Summer Taylor-Braddon: No—don't try and interrupt. You'll get your chance later. Let me speak.

My voice *will* be heard.

Everyone wanted to be here for it. The first meeting. The reunion. Me and my love, united after years apart, when my beloved had been assumed dead.

My mother squeezed my knee so hard while we waited. Later I found bruises had formed like cobweb kisses across my skin. I stared at those bruises in the days that followed. Watched them turn from yellow to black to purple, then fade to ghosts until there was nothing left. Like my whole life.

"This will all be over soon," Mum murmured to me, in her reassuring way.

Of course, she was trying to soothe my anxiety. She's always known how unbearable I find anticipation. How nervous I get. And of course how nervous I'd be for this of all things.

But the papers got her words. People like you, Adelaide, got her words, even though they were a murmur. She was barely audible.

Vultures like you—

Adelaide James: I really—

Summer Taylor-Braddon: No, do *not* interrupt. I am telling my story and this is my story. My perspective.

Vultures like you got all our words, only you also made up your own, too, and pretended they'd fallen from my mouth, my mother's mouth. One paper, not yours—though it may as well have been—had the headline of 'TAYLOR-BRADDON AND MOTHER OVERHEARD PLOTTING MURDER.'

Our room had been bugged. The world was listening in on our conversation—all of it. Annmarie's instructions, my mother's private, comforting words meant only for me, and of course, the reunion when it happened some thirteen minutes later, when Ruari finally arrived here.

[In the background of the audio, car horns can be heard]

Summer Taylor-Braddon: What should've been the most blessed and private moment of my life, being reunited with my husband, was blasted over the media. Every word was analyzed, sentences torn apart and put back together, but badly, so the meaning was changed, because that's your specialty.

Every paper had a different interpretation. *'SUMMER TAYLOR-BRADDON JUST CAN'T LET HER FIRST LOVE GO—EVEN THOUGH HE DOESN'T KNOW WHO SHE IS'* and *'THE WEEPING*

MINX VOWS TO MAKE RUARI BRADDON REMEMBER HER, WHATEVER IT TAKES.'

It wasn't just those headlines that were bad, or indeed the words you'd chosen previously, when the whole nightmare started. Later on, once people like you found out about Mia, you wrote a part for her in the narrative too, painted her as the victim because I could only be the monster, right? 'TAYLOR-BRADDON ADMITS SHE'S GOING TO KILL MIA WILSON.'

Everyone believed at least one of these lies. *Everyone.*

My inboxes and every platform were filled with a deluge of hate.

WE KNOW YOU PLANNED IT ALL!

WHAT KIND OF SICK PERSON ARE YOU?

HOME WRECKER.

There were people I'd gone to school with, even one of my really close friends, poisoned against me. Because of you, they all acted as if they knew exactly what went on in that hotel room, between me and Ruari. They'd listened to the *illegal*—and please note the stress on that word—audio of our conversation, and assumed they knew everything. That's what really annoys me because so much of communication is body language. As a writer, you should know this too. It's how we hold our bodies, it's the expressions on our faces, and it's gestures. But all you had, all the world now had, were the words.

[*She laughs*] I was actually worried that this project we're doing was audio-only, at first. But at least I can control this narrative—and no, before you suggest it, I don't mean that I'll lie. I just mean I'm in control of *my* words getting out. You'll have no chance to edit this, because we're doing each session in one take.

Adelaide James: Are you permitting me to speak yet?

Summer Taylor-Braddon: Your time will come. Be patient. Right now, this is my space. And when I try and recall our conversation in that hotel, mine and Ruari's, I can't actually remember what we said. What we meant or might've meant. I have never wanted to listen to that damn recording, of course. But that whole time, it's… everything leading up to the reunion is almost crystal clear, and so is everything *after* that meeting too. But the meeting itself? Well, all I remember now are the papers' headlines. So I guess you should be proud of yourself.

Adelaide James: I lost my job because of you.

Summer Taylor-Braddon: I lost my life. I think I win, on this. [*She clears her throat*] I hate you all, you know?

Journalists, reporters, press, all the media. You are the predators who enjoy tearing pieces off the nearly dead. And me? I am the most talked about woman in the UK today. And that just seems ridiculous.

But me and Ruari, we're the most talked about couple.

I never wanted fame—I think few novelists do—and though I plan my novels, I do not plot my life. Something on this scale could not have been planned. Ruari and I were victims. *Both* of us.

He did not lie. I did not lie.

Although I have profited from interviews and sponsorships in recent years, we never did this to make money. All we wanted was each other, safe.

So, I'm starting at the beginning—and I do really suggest, Adelaide, that you sit back a bit. You look awfully tense and that can't be good on your back. There—isn't that better?

[Silence for five seconds]

Summer Taylor-Braddon: Ruari and I met in 2010. We were fourteen. He'd just transferred to Okehampton College. He'd been at Budehaven Community School, before that, and it was mid-May when he transferred. We were in year 10, so no exams that year for us, but it gave us only a couple months before the summer holidays. I'd like to say that we became friends right away, only we didn't.

He was average looking, then. Neither skinny nor overweight. Neither tall nor short. Mousy brown hair. Blue eyes. He hadn't yet grown into his face or lost the baby fat that he'd have until his early twenties when he really started to shine.

He was just a quiet, studious boy. I didn't really take any notice of him, barely talked to him, apart from that project in biology. Growing seeds. Can't remember the type now, but we had to water them. Measure them twice a day. Had several sets of them too. Some were over fed, some near drowned, some locked in the dark.

I don't really remember much about it.

But anyway, I'm going further back than when I met Ruari.

So, who am I? Well, I'm the youngest daughter of Margaret Taylor. My mum's my best friend. Always there for me. She's sick now, she's got kidney failure. But she's still here for me. Always.

And she got me legal representation and everything—because she used to be a lawyer. She stopped when she had me and my sister. That's Matilda. She's the model, the one who the papers have been printing those risqué photos of, ever since my story came to light, as if Matilda's job somehow discredits my experiences.

Adelaide James: The public deserves to know the truth.

Summer Taylor-Braddon: Matilda's ten years older than me, and she moved out when I was seven-and-a-half. No, I was nearly eight years old, I think. It had been the three of us, growing up. A house near Fatherford Lane in Okehampton. So then it was just me and Mum. I want to say 'rattling' around in that house, but there was never any rattling because that implies empty space and hard surfaces. It was a small house, but it was perfect for us. Always warm, inviting, cozy. We had this super soft carpet—a light pink color, and it was so wonderful to walk barefoot on it.

Mum worked two part-time jobs once I was old enough and at school. Not law. Cleaning. Mum always said she hated it, but she did what she needed to do to put food on the table. And from about when I was eight or nine, we'd get some money from Mattie too. She'd send some back when she had really well-paying jobs. We weren't like super poor, but we weren't always comfortable.

Sugar sandwiches, in my lunch box until the school realized, said it wasn't nutritious. They suggested cheese or tuna, and Mum was in tears then. *Do they think I'd be giving you sugar if I had a choice?*

But after that, I did have cheese.

Mum stopped eating some meals though. I didn't know this until later. Still feel bad now though.

[*Neither Summer nor Adelaide speak for five seconds, but traffic can be heard nearby*]

Summer Taylor-Braddon: It's what mothers do right? Sacrifice. [*She clears her throat*] But yeah, even though there's my sister, it often was just me and Mum, all through my teenage years. And my friends all loved Mum. Hana and Julia, they were my besties. And when we got into Sixth Form, our friendship group kind of merged with the boys—Ruari and his two friends. Dante and Ashley. We became a six. We hung out in the park together in free lessons or after school. We were at my house a lot, too. Didn't really go to their homes much. Mainly it was Mum. Mum loved them all. Loved having a full house, she said.

She'd always wanted more kids. Of course, she was entirely devoted to Dad. When he got killed—he was a soldier, Afghanistan—I was three. But she never dated again. So no more kids. But she sort of 'adopted' my friends. And Ruari.

And she *was* concerned about him. She really listened to him, asked what she could do to help. She'd sit with him at our kitchen table. You see, he was having a tough time at home. That was why he really liked coming to my house. He gradually opened up about this, when it was the whole group of us and Mum, but also when it was just me and Mum and him.

He'd sit there, breathing deeply, his hand trembling. "I just… I don't know why she does it," he told me.

You see, he was talking about his mum, and his blue eyes darkened to this steel grey—the hue they went when he was really troubled by something. I only met Portia a couple of times, before she died. An overdose. She'd struggled with addiction for years, and Ruari, as her only child, had struggled too. I'd noticed, of course I had, that he'd been coming to school later and later, many mornings turning up with huge bags under his eyes. His clothes were getting more thread-bare and several times he only had a quarter of a sandwich in his lunchbox from home. He'd eat it really quickly too, sort of looking around at everyone, as if daring anyone to make a comment about it.

He didn't have money for school trips. There weren't even that many, in Sixth Form, but there socials. These nights that our Sixth Form committee would put on, but he didn't go on a lot of them.

When our friendship group was hanging out, we always tried to do things that didn't cost anything, because none of us really ever talked to him about it—until I did.

We were seventeen. At the end of year 12. Ruari and I both had a free lesson before Assembly, whereas Hana and Dante were in Chemistry, Ashley in Psychology—or it might've been Media Studies—and Julia had dance. Our group tended to hang out in the little computer room in the Sixth-Form block, and I was sitting at a table, the computer keyboard pushed back so there was room for my bag and folder. I was going through my notes from English Lit, and he came in. He stopped a few spaces away from me, sat heavily in the chair, like the weight of the world was on his shoulders, and I tried not to look at him.

But of course I glanced up. "All right?" I asked.

"Yep," he replied, his voice curt, and he just stared at the computer in front of him. The machine was off. The screen black, reflecting his face. I could only see that all distorted though, because of the angle, and when I looked up at him, I was struck by his strong profile.

In the last year or so, he'd filled out a bit. He was now the same height as me, but his face seemed stronger. Harder lines around it, making up its edges, even though he also still had baby fat. His jaw was strong, his nose finally seemed to be the right size for his face and no longer on the large size, and he was clearly in need of a shave. I'd not really paid a lot of attention to Ruari's shaving routine. He always was fresh-faced, soft skin, only now he wasn't. Like he'd not shaven in a day or two. Which was fine—more than fine, really, because it made this part of me want to reach out and touch him.

Only I couldn't because that would've been so, so weird. He was my friend.

But I noticed how attractive he looked. Maybe not in the conventional way. But still, it was a way that really spoke to me.

His glasses had steamed up, upon coming in here, even though it was pretty warm outside, but he took them off now, and that was when I saw it. The faint shadow of a bruise around his eye socket.

Yeah. I said something like, "Oh my God." And it didn't seem enough, you know? I was standing up, heading over to him before I'd even realized I was doing it. "Are you okay? What's happened?" I couldn't believe I'd not seen it before, to be honest, because it didn't really look new.

But my mind flashed back to last week—when he'd been off. Measles, he'd told us all. He'd only just come back the day before, in fact. I'd not really seen him much that day though—Mondays were my busiest of days—but sitting there, in the computer room, I felt… I don't know. Overwhelmed with it all.

He looked up at me—I was still hovering over him—and he slumped farther back in his seat, then slowly put his glasses back on. His Adam's apple bobbed a bit as he visibly swallowed. "I'm just so tired, Summer." His voice even sounded tired, like huge weights were sitting on the words, dragging them down.

I sat next to him, very aware that my breathing was fast. I leant forward, propping my elbows on the computer desk, and looked carefully at him. He met my eyes slowly, and then it all just poured out.

He told me about his mother's new boyfriend. A man named Al. Al had come over several times before and Ruari didn't like him. Al was too quick with his fists.

"At first it was just Mum," he told me, "just her being hit. When I wasn't there. But…" He shook his head. "Last week." His breaths shook—like, so loudly. "I thought I could help her, but she… she sided with him. Kicked me out."

My eyes widened. "Kicked you out?"

He looked down at his hands. He had a hangnail on one finger, and I watched as he appeared to steel himself before he tore it off. He flinched as he did it though, and it made me feel sick, imagining it all. The pain.

"Where are you staying?" I asked. I was worried my tone had come out too harsh, but he just looked at me with soft eyes and shook his head. And it was that thought—of Ruari sleeping in a back garden somewhere, or a doorway or a gutter—that really made me feel so, so sick. I reached out, placed my hand over his. His skin was cold. "We've got a spare room," I said, even though Mum was always telling me not to call it a spare room. It was Matilda's, even if recently when she'd visited she'd chosen to stay in hotels in Exeter. Said that was easier for her work.

"No, I can't," Ruari said. "I…" His face crumpled.

"No arguments. You're staying with us."

So, that's what happened.

Mum really liked Ruari. I think she knew that me and him were going to get together before we actually did. I mean, we were getting on well, and he did live with us for a bit, until Social Services sorted things out for him. They managed to get hold of his dad—apparently he'd just been released from prison, not that I'd even known back then that he had been inside—but then his mum ended things with Al, and Ruari did go back home.

I was worried at first. So was Mum. I kept messaging him, talking to him, and he did still come over to my house a lot. He said he felt calmer here, and I know he never really wanted to move out. But he also felt incredibly guilty about putting my mum to the trouble—he told me this once.

Anyway, Ruari and I started dating that summer we left Sixth Form, not that we really put a name to it at first, but we'd started seeing each other more. When Hana, Julia, Dante, and Ashley would leave my house, Ruari would find an excuse to stay a bit later. But it was different than when he was living with us, for those two months. Then, I'd been there for him, but I was… I don't know how to describe it. Well, I was trying to think of him as a brother, even though such a huge part of me often wanted to reach out and hold his hands. I'd want to hug him, hold him, as soon as I saw him.

I just wanted to be there for him. Reassure him.

But when it was that summer, and he began hanging around at my house more than the rest of our friends, I felt the shift in the air. The change. We'd sit on the patio. I'd be painting my toenails or something and he'd just watch me, smiling. When I painted my fingernails, he'd do my left hand for me and he'd take really great care with it too, frowning a little as he did so. I must admit, I loved it when he painted my nails. Loved his touch on me, the soft and careful way he held my hands, yet his grip was also firm, certain, reassuring.

And we'd be sitting so close. So close I could just reach across, rest my head on his shoulder, or kiss him.

I *wanted* to kiss him. I really did. But I was… well, nervous. What if he thought we were just friends?

And I didn't want to risk things by making the first move and getting it so, so wrong.

But we'd go to the cinema together. Just the two of us, without telling our friends. It felt special, magical. It was us. And it felt like a date.

We finally had our first kiss on August 9th 2013. That was… well, I almost don't want to tell you. It feels too personal, you know? Like, I'm being expected to share so much of me. Leave nothing untold, no stone unturned. Who else in the world is that expected of?

I mean I want to keep some things for me. But I also know that the public really wants to know. And people like you think that I don't deserve privacy.

It's the curse of being an author too. People think they're entitled to every part of my story. [*She laughs.*] I just wish they'd understand that my books are fiction, but my life is… well. It's mine.

Anyway, I wanted to do this project with you to not just make people understand, but to tell you why you're wrong. To argue with you—and to win. You may smile, Adelaide, but I know what I'm doing. And in doing this, I've kind of given up any right to privacy. All the covers are being stripped back.

So, mine and Ruari's first kiss. Begin early with something romantic—hook everyone.

It was at a bus stop, near the top of Okehampton. Not that romantic, but maybe we can spin it that way.

He was getting on a bus, and I was waiting with him. As the bus trundled into sight, in a long line of traffic, I turned to say goodbye to him. The stop itself wasn't busy, we were the only ones there. I went to hug him—as I often did—and that's when it happened.

His lips, soft, brushed mine. I gasped a little, feeling electricity whizz through my body. My knees suddenly felt weak—that old cliche—and then I kissed him back.

To be honest, it was a pretty chaste kiss. Neither of us were that experienced or anything. But it was perfect for us.

[Four seconds of silence]

Summer Taylor-Braddon: Anyway, a few weeks later, our A-level results came in. A Thursday morning. Terrible weather. I'd been supposed to meet Julia and Hana at the dry cleaners' shop down the bottom of Oke, and we were going to walk up together. But when I got there—absolutely soaked, because I'd walked down the massive hill in the pouring rain, I found Julia and Hana had already left. Hana's mum worked in the shop. That's why we'd chosen to meet there. Take the final walk to school together. But it didn't work out like that.

I'd felt more anxious, walking in there on my own. Felt, I don't know, strange. But I'd got into my first place university. Kingston. London.

I still don't know why I actually applied. I mean, I didn't think I'd get in. I applied more as a 'may as well' kind of thing. But I got in.

Ruari wasn't going to uni though. That was the problem.

And it couldn't work though, he realized, when I would be away in London. How could it? He asked that, over and over again. And that was when I knew we had our first communication problem. Because being long distance appealed a whole lot more to me, for one reason only: less chance of us sleeping together.

You've got to understand, back then, I didn't know about the ace spectrum. I thought I was just… I don't know. Scared. Broken. Like there was something wrong with me. I just assumed that sex was this thing that I'd have to do eventually, once he and I had been 'together' a little longer. The cost of being in love.

And I knew—or at least I thought I did—that he wanted to be doing it. He told me later that he *thought* he wanted to, because he *thought* that was what he should've been doing. And he thought that I would want to, too. His friends were constantly asking him whether we'd done it yet. He'd already told me this, and I thought that was his way of testing whether I was ready.

I was not ready, and I felt pathetic that I was eighteen years old and I didn't want to have sex with him. But I also didn't want to lose him. But me going off to London, well, it seemed like it would solve the problem—even though I didn't want to lose him.

You've got to understand, he was my first love. My only love. Things just clicked between us, as cliché as that sounds.

But we ended up breaking up just before I went off to London, and I was utterly heartbroken. Duvet days, being the saddo who eats the whole tub of Ben & Jerry's, day after day. And of course, it was the start of uni, too. Freshers' Week. I didn't go out though. Didn't take part in the activities, the clubbing, the free society taster sessions. I just couldn't stop crying, couldn't stop hiding away.

I felt pathetic, being that upset over a guy. But it was Ruari. It felt different with him. You see, I'd kissed a few boys before. Gone on dates. But they always felt… I don't know. Performative. Prescriptive. Whereas with Ruari, it was right. Organic. Yes, that's the word. And we started off as friends. We knew each other before we got together, so we just felt… right.

But we'd both thought, at the end of that summer, that there was no way it could work. So, that was it.

But of course, it wasn't. Spoilers! But everyone knows.

Anyway, now it's time to bring a few other people into the studio.

[Sounds of a door opening, people entering and sitting down, and the door closing]

Summer Taylor-Braddon: Firstly, thank you so much, everyone, for coming into the studio at the weekend—I really do appreciate it. And I know it hasn't been easy to find a time when you're all free.

So, three guests have joined us. Would you like to introduce yourselves?

Hana Burton: My name is Hana Burton. I'm Summer's *best* friend.

Julia Rivers: Julia. We, uh, were friends.

Ashley Kincade: And I'm Ashley.

Adelaide James: We hadn't agreed on others coming into the first session.

Summer Taylor-Braddon: If only I talked, people would accuse me of lying. Bringing in more voices makes it better, right? Anyway, don't get jealous. You'll have a chance next week to bring in whoever you want—if you're still on talking terms with them?

Anyway, thank you for coming in, Hana, Ashley, and Julia. So I've just got to the point where Ruari and

I broke up, just when I was leaving for university. I'd like to stick to a roughly chronological timeline for everything if we can, so can you tell us about this?

Hana Burton: Well, uh, I was surprised. Like, really. You and him, you'd seemed so perfect for each other. Like, when we were at school, you just started getting closer and closer, and it was obvious to all of us that you were meant to be together.

You'd sort of do this—we called it 'their dance'. Not an actual dance. Sorry—I don't know who I direct this to. Direct address of third person.

Summer Taylor-Braddon: How about you pretend I'm not here and just talk to the viewer?

Hana Burton: Okay, so it's like if Summer came into the room, Ruari would turn his body toward her. Wherever she walked, he'd turn to face her. And the same with her too. They were, like, drawn to each other. So aware of where each other was, even if it was subconscious.

Julia Rivers: We thought they'd have got together in year 12, but it took a bit longer. Was really great when they were though—even if they thought they'd hidden it from us well enough.

Ashley Kincade: Yeah, there was no hiding it. They were just meant to be together. And that's why we were all surprised when they called things off.

He was proper cut up about it, too. I mean, I'd assumed it had been Summer's decision, but he said that he'd made the choice—seemed to think it was the best thing. Yet he talked about her nonstop after. Proper lamenting. We were worried about him.

Hana Burton: Summer didn't—talk about him, that is. I mean, Julia and I tried to get her to talk—we were worried about her, too, you know? But she just closed up completely. We didn't really hear much from her after she went away to London.

Adelaide James: And what about you, Julia?

Julia Rivers: We figured she was moving on. Like, she was tagged in so many photos of nights out, so we thought she was doing okay. She looked like she was having fun.

Ashley Kincade: Ruari wasn't though. He told me he shouldn't have let her get away like that. He should've held onto her. He was… he sort of became colder. Before, he'd always laugh, but he didn't. Not in the year that followed. Whenever he and I met up—which,

I mean, we tried to do every month—there was always this wall up around him. It felt like he was keeping me at a distance, and I knew he was hurting. But I didn't really try hard enough to get him to talk. I mean, we're blokes. We kicked a football around, drank pints in the pub, but we never really talked.

But I knew. Of course I knew. Everyone who looked at him knew.

Hana Burton: The thing about Ruari is that he's vulnerable. He always has been, but he's not the type of person to open up about it.

Ashley Kincade: Not to us anyway. It's the kind of thing he would've told Summer about—you know, if it wasn't her that he'd broken up with. If it had been some other girl. Because those two, they'd been so, so close.

But then he, like—well, it was almost like he had no one.

He started drinking more and more. I'm not saying he was an alcoholic or anything, but he definitely liked a drink. We'd usually have a couple pints, you know, when we met up, but I remember one time—I think it was March, maybe late March—and I arrived at the pub and he'd already been drinking there for a while, that was obvious. He had all these empty glasses on his table, and he looked kind of sheepish. Embarrassed. You know, that I'd seen them.

But he still ordered two more, maybe three.

Julia Rivers: He called me once, when he was really drunk. Like, slurring his words.

Hana Burton: He did?

Julia Rivers: Yeah. I'm still not sure why. I couldn't really make out what he was saying. I just messaged Ash and Dante about it. Figured you'd make sure he was okay. It wasn't like the six of us hung out anymore.

Adelaide James: And was Ruari okay?

Ashley Kincade: Don't know. I didn't get that message until later, from Jules. And by then, I think Dante had gone round his house. *[He sighs]* Honestly, I was having my own relationship problems. This girl I'd met a few months ago. We'd had a massive row. And so when I got the message from Jules, I just didn't really take it in. It didn't seem important to me.

But, I mean, it was fine. Not like he'd done anything stupid.

Hana Burton: It doesn't feel right, talking about him like this. It doesn't feel right talking about any of this…

Summer Taylor-Braddon: Do you want to stop?

Hana Burton: I… I don't know. I don't want to speak ill of him. I mean, we shouldn't, right? But Ruari wasn't right then. He was a mess. Drunk most of the time. My mum thought he was buying drugs, too.

Ashley Kincade: No, he wouldn't have done that.

Julia Rivers: Well, we don't know, do we?

Ashley Kincade: All we know is that Ruari was a mess back then. He really needed Summer.

Summer Taylor-Braddon: Okay, thank you—that helps set the scene. I will take over again now. [*Sounds of papers shuffling*] So, Ruari and I reconnected a year later. It was the summer of 2014, and I was close to dropping out of university, finding that academia just wasn't right for me. He'd just finished an apprenticeship. And it was all totally unexpected—for both of us.

[*She takes a deep breath*] It was stormy that day, and I—I still find it weird talking about this. Because this is part of the story where it's all about my sexuality and… I just feel like, I'm 'outing' myself again. Though of course it's not like when you did that for me, is it,

Adelaide? What? No comment here? Cat got your tongue? Wow.

Hana Burton: Uh, Summer, do you want us to leave, if you're talking about this?

Summer Taylor-Braddon: Nah, it's fine. But, see, Adelaide? That's what decent people do. They think of others.

Anyway, the advisors I spoke to recommended that you were all here when I talk about this for the first time. They said that because asexuality is not often talked about and there's an air of mystery about it, that it would come across—what was it? More authentic? If I spoke about it casually for the first time in this project, with friends present. That then it wouldn't seem like this big secret or something that should be hidden away and not talked about in front of others.

Ashley Kincade: As long as you don't get too soppy on us with your love story. [*He laughs*]

Summer Taylor-Braddon: [*She clears her throat*] So, in the last year in London, I'd started to find out about queer spaces, because my roommate Charlotte had joined the LGBTQIA+ society at uni, and she'd dragged me along to the socials. I learned about asexuality at one of them, from a pretty cool guy with spiky purple hair. And I started wondering, *Is this me?*

With the first year of my undergrad studies out the way, I returned to Devon, dropped my suitcase off at Mum's new house—she'd just had to move because the downstairs had flooded, but the landlord had another property vacant that she could move into—and so there I was, arriving at this strange new house. She'd left the key under the mat at the back of the house for me, and although I'd seen photos of which would be my room, it didn't seem right for me to go and settle myself in. I needed to be shown.

I had about an hour before I guessed she'd get in, and so I sat at the kitchen table, my phone in hand. It was reassuring, seeing the familiar marks on the kitchen table—ink stains and water rings from mugs of hot drinks placed on the wax surface when one of us had forgotten to use a coaster—but it was also eerie. Looking at the pale-yellow tiles over the sink. The much bigger room. The built-in fridge and dishwasher with their matching aluminum finishes. It didn't feel like home, so I did the thing I'd grown accustomed to doing of late, when I was anxious.

I was Googling on my phone, and I'd been researching more and more about asexuality, feeling like it was a safe and welcoming space that might just help me. Might explain me. I wasn't broken. But I was still skeptical, reluctant to use the word. Probably because of the negative connotations—I'd seen some talk of it in the forums. How people laughed at asexual people, sometimes. Saw us as plant-like, not human. Something wrong with us.

Wrong with our thinking, our feelings.

I don't really know what made me do it, but I found an ace dating site, while sitting in this kitchen that both felt familiar and not, and ten minutes later, I'd made a profile. Filled out a little info. I was still feeling embarrassed though, so I didn't use my real name as my username. I was Folkloric Girl. I still don't know why I chose that. But I intentionally chose a pretty blurry photo, worried that someone in real life would see it, recognize me, and know my secret.

Then Mum was back, and it was all hugs and kisses and coffee-making and *Summer, you really must try one of these Danishes I just picked up.* My new room was pretty cool, too. Mum had unpacked my things for me and it looked like a back-to-front version of my old room.

I liked it, and I thought that the summer holidays might be okay. A couple months here, while I decided what to do—if I would be going back to Kingston.

Of course, I was going to be avoiding Ruari. Julia and Hana knew that. That was a given. We'd decided we wouldn't be meeting with any of the guys. Just the girls, again. But my friends weren't back yet. Hana was going to Disney Land Florida with her family and Julia was visiting somewhere in Italy with her roommates from uni. She'd shared halls with some pretty posh kids, and they'd even paid for her plane tickets out there.

So this gave me two weeks to myself. Just me and Mum. A chance for me to decompress and decide what I was going to do. I really didn't want to go back to Kingston in the autumn. In fact, I couldn't really think of anything I dreaded more—other than bumping into Ruari in the Post Office or the Co-op or something.

Mum and I drew up so many pros and cons charts that summer, about uni, staying at Kingston, leaving, transferring somewhere closer, doing a different course, taking a gap year—I didn't even know that was possible mid-studies, but apparently it is. Just called something else though.

And it was mid-August, just as we were about to go out to go and meet Hana and her mum for coffee, when I got the notification from the ace dating site. Someone had liked my profile. Someone had sent me a message.

My heart pounded, because as soon as I saw the username, I knew. GraniteMan. Oh, I haven't told you yet about that—so Ruari was obsessed with Dartmoor. He'd done Ten Tors when we were at school and his

Duke of Edinburgh awards had involved hiking on the moors too. He'd become really fascinated with rocks and geology, and we spent a few days in the local museums, researching it all too. I'd light-heartedly called him 'Granite Man' and then it had kind of stuck.

So, when I saw this username, of course I thought it was him.

I felt so sick as I clicked onto the message.

Fancy seeing you on here.

I flushed too hot, then too cold. My clothes suddenly felt too small, too tight around my abdomen, and my underarms and back were slick with sweat.

Was this a joke? Were he and his mates laughing at me, having found out my deepest secret? The one secret I wasn't ready to share with anyone. Because, well, I still didn't quite understand it myself. I still felt embarrassed.

This is what you get for putting it online though, the voice in my head told me.

I didn't reply to him. I convinced myself that it wasn't him. That it was some other person from school, someone pretending to be him, playing a joke on me. Other people must have found out that I called him Granite Man.

But the next day, he messaged me again. He asked why I'd blocked him on Facebook and Instagram—I hadn't, I just had deleted my accounts. It was too painful seeing him tagged in photos—expeditions and walks on the moor, training days with the army, coffee catchups, that sort of thing. He was asking why I'd deleted him though. He was always so full of questions.

I ignored his messages on the dating site—until I couldn't. Him, in the doorway of Mum's new house. Looking, so… the same. There was light misty rain sitting in his dark hair, on the lenses of his glasses. He looked a little taller than I'd remembered. I'd always thought we were the same height, but apparently he was now about two inches taller than me.

He'd also changed his style of clothes. I loved how he'd wear band shirts before, with dark jeans and chunky army-style boots. But now he was dressed more smartly. Not a suit, but casual smart. And I realized I didn't know what he was doing now. For work, for fun, if he was with someone.

Seeing him again was like a huge chasm inside me was opening up, ripping my insides apart. I gasped and gasped, and yet his first words were, "You look well," before he then laughed and said how formal that sounded.

I didn't think I looked at all well, because I was pretty sure I was having some sort of asthma attack. I grabbed hold of the doorframe to steady myself and a splinter dug into the fleshy pad of my thumb. I pulled my hand back quick, eyes focused on the shard of wood, because that was easier—anything was easier—than looking at him.

As I carefully, cautiously, pulled the splinter out, I summoned up the courage to speak. Because it was courage—that was what I needed just to speak to him. "What do you want?" My voice shook.

"You," he said simply, and I guess I knew that this was the moment. The romantic moment in some many romcoms and heartfelt romantic films where the couple finally realize that they need to be together. That they can't live without each other.

I don't remember which of us moved first. But then we were touching, hugging. His arms locked around me and I breathed in his scent—his deodorant hadn't changed—and being with him, well, it felt like home.

We didn't kiss or anything. No hands roaming under clothes. It was… chaste. Sweet.

I invited him in. We sat six feet apart in my mother's living room, separate chairs for Mum had had to get new ones. The sofa that Ruari and I had snuggled up on in the old house and been damaged by the flood. I stared at Ruari's feet as we sat there. He'd taken his shoes off and his socks had a hole in.

"How're your parents doing?" I asked.

Hurt flashed onto his face, just for a second, but it was enough. Then he shook his head. A smile plastered its way across his face. "Good."

I've always known when he's lying. Always. And I told him that, and he just… well, he crumpled.

I don't know which of us moved first, again, but we met in the middle of the living room, reaching for each other.

"It will be okay," I whispered, as I held him, as he held me.

"It will be okay," he said.

[*She clears her throat*] We fell in love, again, quick, hard. And it was easier this time, like we were on the same page. It helped that we had, technically, reconnected on the ace dating site. We both knew each other's secret.

I mean, at first, I had still been cautious. Wondered if he really was. Because I guess all the toxic masculinity ideas had really got to me and I was looking at Ruari, wondering how someone who looked so masculine with his beard, so full of testosterone, could well, not be interested in sex.

He spoke about it once, a few months later, how he hadn't been sure, thought he was broken. That he even went to the doctor. That they offered him therapy. It made him feel like less of a man, until he went to the therapist and was told nothing was wrong with him. Being asexual is not being broken. It's not being wrong. It's not being abnormal.

Being asexual is natural.

"We must've known, both of us before," he said, that day in my mum's new living room. "Subconsciously. We're just meant to be together."

It was easy after that. I didn't have to be worried, didn't feel like I'd inevitably be pressured into sleeping with him to keep him. It was just such a huge relief. We'd found each other, and we were the same.

September was coming around though, and I knew I needed to make a decision about whether I was going back to London. Ruari was now working in the Museum of Dartmoor Life, in Okehampton, and I wanted nothing more than to stay here. But Mum did keep saying that I couldn't stay for a boy. That Ruari was a decent boy and he'd wait for me.

But I didn't know if I wanted to go back. I didn't want to put distance between us again, because it was unlikely he'd be able to afford to travel to London to see me. His mum was in a rehab program, but his dad had moved back in with him. Mr. Braddon was drinking a lot, barely working, and all of Ruari's income was going to keep their household afloat.

I didn't want to put pressure on Ruari to spend money on train tickets or driving lessons, but I knew that I wouldn't be able to come back every weekend to see him too. And the thought of not seeing him, of us being apart for any longer, really tore through me. It felt like a gaping wound inside me.

So I suspended my studies.

I moved back home, full-time. I got a job, waitressing in a café in Red Lion Yard.

And I started writing too. Mainly because I was bored at first, during the times when I'd be waiting for Ruari to finish work. I started writing these stories. Just silly little things. I hadn't really written or read much outside of academic work when I'd been at university, but this really allowed me to find myself again, my love for stories.

Over the next few months, years even, life was perfect. It was November 2015 when I got an agent for my books. Six months later, she phoned me to say she'd got a publisher who was really interested. I had a call with the acquisitions editor, and I actually felt like I could be a proper writer. I'd already decided then that I'd hyphenate mine and Ruari's names, for my pen name—Summer Taylor-Braddon—as there was already a Summer Taylor writing, and it felt so exciting. Just knowing, you know? Some people find that weird that I chose to use both our names like that, before we were married—before he'd proposed. But we knew we were going to be together. We knew it in our souls.

And a week later, my agent had the deal memo come through for my first book. This was *Swept Away*. Contract negotiations began, and then five months later, I was able to sign the contract and announce the deal.

I was going to be a traditionally published author, and nothing felt better than that. Well, that and having my life sorted. Being with Ruari. My man.

I think that's the happiest time of my life. Those few years. Because Ruari and I moved in together pretty quickly too—first into Mum's house in 2015, then into our own flat in 2016. It was on the road to the castle, a cottage that had just been converted into three different flats. We had the top floor, but also a room at the bottom of the cottage that had its own staircase, so we had our own front door there too. It was pretty cool. And of course it was really close to where Ruari was then working—at the castle itself. I guess I should explain about the castle too.

So it's the ruins of a medieval motte and bailey castle. I think it was built some time in the eleventh century. It's now managed by English Heritage, and that's how Ruari started working there. At first, I think he was just doing tours of the grounds for visitors, but then he got more involved in English Heritage's other historical sites on Dartmoor. He'd got his driver's license by then, so often he was leaving quite early in the mornings, out on the moors for most of the day. There was an archaeological dig or something going on at Grimspound, and he was so excited to be able to work on that. It wasn't exactly geology—or what he'd thought he'd want to do—but it was Dartmoor, and it really got him into prehistory. Bronze Age stuff. He did these, uh, YouTube videos about it, and they actually really took off. Like, loads of people were watching them.

He started an online archaeology degree, and I've honestly never seen him light up so much. It was amazing—his enthusiasm was contagious. That's why one of the protagonists in one of my books ended up being an archaeologist. It was kind of like this joint project that Ruari and I had going on. And it was great. The flat wasn't that big, but we had a second bedroom, and at that point, while we were working on that book, we had it as an office. A massive table in there—almost as big as the room itself, and we could only just fit in two chairs. We'd have all these archaeology and Dartmoor books piled up on the table, and notebooks everywhere, and we'd both work there. Me writing, and Ruari studying.

We were so happy in that flat. Yeah, we lived there for, well, all the time until… well, until he went missing. I couldn't really go back there after what had happened, so I moved back into Mum's, but sorry, I'm jumping ahead, aren't I?

Hana Burton: Well, perhaps now would be a good time to ask you more about romance when you're asexual? I know when we talked yesterday, you mentioned some things that you specifically wanted to address. And you told me to ask you them.

Adelaide James: Hold on, *I'm* the interviewer here.

Summer Taylor-Braddon: Yes, well you are *an* interviewer—but I don't exactly want you of all people asking me these questions—and I believe you'd already got a lot of things you want to talk about later. But like I said, this is my session today. I'm leading it. You'll get to talk on Monday.

So, the misconceptions about what asexuality is and isn't—because people often think that you can't be truly in love if you don't have sex. Or if you don't experience sexual attraction. They see us as… lacking.

I am going to tell you about specific occasions.

So, setting the scene: We were lying in bed, one morning, semi-naked, cuddling. People always assume I mean something sexual by this, but it both is and it isn't. We were barely clothed, and feeling Ruari's skin against mine felt good—so reassuring and safe and calming—and I just wanted that closeness. That feeling of security. And the pressure of his body against mine was like an antidote I never knew I needed. Skin-to-skin contact, like, it's always really made me feel safe.

"I love you," I whispered to him. It wasn't the first time we'd said it, but I still got goosebumps at the way it made me feel, voicing this declaration, cementing this bond that we had.

He smiled, made a pleased sound in the back of his throat, and then kissed me. I shut my eyes as we kissed, as the kiss got deeper and deeper, and his hands roamed over my hips. I rubbed his back, and we were pressing against each other so hard, like we could truly melt into one another.

I was completely and irrevocably in love with him. And it's weird how I always thought about that, when we were kissing, when we were cuddling in bed like this—how certain I'd feel. When, maybe just hours before, watching TV on the sofa or maybe the next morning, eating breakfast, I'd think about what love was and worry whether this was it. Was I feeling it in a correct way? Was it supposed to be something more? Something exciting?

I read a romance novel once that really made a big deal of the instant attraction between the main couple. How the girl had that 'spotlight' moment where she just zeroed-in on the guy who'd be her love interest. How she couldn't wait to touch him, to hold him, to kiss him. How complete she felt just seeing him, knowing that he existed.

I can't pretend that I don't still worry about this—that I've never had a moment like that. Even with Ruari, it's been slow to build, from security and stability and friendship. That trust wasn't instant. I didn't fall in love with him at fourteen years old, even though everyone refers to us as high school sweethearts. And I never had that 'spotlight' moment, where it feels like a light has been shone on him and everything else has dimmed in comparison.

But then I remember what those books are describing: sexual attraction. And I'm asexual. Ruari's asexual. What we have is enough, and it is real, and it is ours, and there's not a wrong way for us to be in love because I know that we are in love, I feel it, even when we're not cuddling in bed.

Even now, knowing that he and I cannot be together anymore—that too much has happened, Mia has happened—I still know I am deeply in love with him.

I still have the same worries—and at twenty-three, I knew I was in a healthy relationship when my biggest worry was that something would happen to him. That Ruari would die. That he'd go for a long drive to visit his family and he'd have an accident. That I'd get a knock on the door, answer it to find a policeman. Maybe two. Hats in hand, somber eyes.

"I'm so sorry, miss," the policeman would say. Or maybe it would be a policewoman. They'd look at me with sad, sad eyes, and I'd gulp and I'd know.

They'd ask if they could come in. I'd show them into the living room. It would be too hot, and I'd be sweating as they'd make me sit down.

"I am afraid I have some bad news to tell you."

Their eyes would be so so sad, and I'd see it all in my head—really play it out, this whole scenario. It would make my chest hurt and my heart hurt and my soul hurt. Whenever I thought about it, I'd feel it like it was real. My eyes would mist up and sometimes I'd actually cry. Sometimes I'd get a huge pain in my head, and it would feel like my insides were crumbling.

I knew at twenty-three I could not live without Ruari.

I needed him. I couldn't be without him.

I was going to spend the rest of my life with him.

Then Ruari proposed. January 2017. It was actually the day before *Swept Away* released. And that was the start of it all—the Hell that followed.

But anyway, we'll take a quick break now.

Summer Taylor-Braddon: So, Ashley, Hana, and Julia have left now. It's just me and you, Adelaide—and don't worry, you will get the whole stage, shortly. Or the whole studio. But let me just finish this part.

So, it wasn't Hell immediately. Of course not. Ruari and I were in love. And it felt so exciting, knowing that we were making this commitment, that we'd be life-long partners. That we'd grow old together. That I had truly found my person.

There were still so many times, back then, when I couldn't believe it. When I just stopped and looked at Ruari—this handsome man who was perfect for me, who I was perfect for. I had found him. I mean, what are the chances?

But we had found each other, and we did everything together. He'd always been into geology and stuff and we began going to conventions on that for him. Conferences. Lectures. That sort of stuff. And for me, we'd go to book fairs. He'd sit through long talks by authors he'd never heard of, but he'd appear to be interested, and then he'd talk to me about it all on the way home, engaging in conversation—just as I did with him.

We set a date for our wedding—5th July, that same year, 2017. We had six months leading up to it, and I remember the giddy excitement of it all. Because it was exciting, planning a wedding. Looking around venues, picking out table pieces, talking color themes, and of course dress shopping.

Hana and Julia went with me to my first wedding dress appointment. I'd wanted Mum to come but she had work. She'd already booked the week off for the wedding itself but her boss was being a bit of a dick really and wouldn't let her take any time off beforehand. "Anyway, I'll get to one of the fitting appointments," she told me. "Once you have your dress."

Julia created a Pinterest board especially for wedding dresses. This was of course when she and I were still friends. The three of us started watching all sorts of bride-chooses-her-dress programs and Hana would clog up my IG inbox with reel after reel.

"You should totally get a dress that's a bit different," she said one day when the three of us were lounging on my bed. "You're like, goth. Your dress should be."

I hadn't been 'goth' in years—that was like, in year 7 and 8 at school—but I guess I still had those edgy vibes. Still listened to My Chemical Romance and Avril Lavigne, still watched a lot of horror films, still was drawn to reading dark fiction. "But I want a traditional dress," I said. "White all the way."

Julia rolled her eyes, and sure, she did keep trying to get me to look at different styles of dresses, but I held firm. Anyway, beyond the dress being white and traditional—or maybe even somewhat traditional—I wasn't truly sure what I wanted. If I'm being honest, I was just so overwhelmed as we looked through image after image, video after video.

"I like the skirt there," I said.

"That's the train." Hana rolled her eyes. "Anyway, what kind of neckline do you like?"

I gestured at my own body and sort of traced a pattern on my T-shirt. "Like this?" I had no idea what any of these necklines were called, but Hana nodded, said I was describing a boat neck, and then started typing that into Google.

There were so many parts to dress design, that's what I discovered. Not just neck lines, but the height of the waist, whether it clinches in around your hips or whirls out, how many layers the skirt has, the kind of materials and textures you're going for, whether you've got sleeves or not, a back of a dress or not—and I was totally shocked when I realized that quite a lot of wedding dresses don't have backs.

"But if I was wearing that and sitting on a stool and there was like a table behind me and someone was behind that table looking at me, if would look like I've got nothing on," I said. "It would look like I was naked!"

Julia laughed and Hana rolled her eyes.

"No, I want a back. I mean, for the amount I'm paying for this dress—it better have a back. Otherwise it's just an extortionate amount for what is essentially a scrap of fabric."

I got better at looking at wedding dresses, at understanding what I liked and what I didn't like—mermaid was the silhouette I thought most flattered me, and I wanted minimal lace, and no sleeves—so by the time we actually got around to booking dress appointments I was able to give the women there a pretty good idea of what I wanted.

It was pouring with rain, when Hana drove the three of us to Exeter. We parked outside The House That Moved, where Pirouette Bridal was based, and I remember looking up at the Tudor-style building and thinking just WOW. It was impressive, and I loved it, and I just felt that my dress was inside there.

We were ten minutes early so we decided to wait in the car for a little bit, just to see if the rain would stop, but alas it didn't. Hana had spent twenty minutes at my house re-straightening her hair after she'd made the dash from her car to my house, and now she was fretting about it. We had no coats with us—I'm not too sure why, when it had definitely been raining in Okehampton—but we found a plastic bag in one of the seat pockets and she fashioned that over her head as a hat.

"This is beautiful," I said as we hovered outside the door—okay, we were trying to work out how to open it. It appeared to be locked.

But then the lady inside saw us and opened the door—apparently very easily—for us. We flocked inside, and I was very aware of how we were dripping water everywhere. Thankfully there were no dresses in the immediate vicinity for us to shed our raindrops on.

"You must be Summer?" the woman asked, with a smile. "I'll just go and get your seamstress."

My seamstress?

I remember feeling like I was stepping into some other world. A world where I had my own seamstress.

It was all pretty cool—and I felt so magical, trying on so many beautiful gowns. The shop had a couple of floors, and there was a dressing room on each floor. I was just upstairs, on the next floor, and it was a pretty small room, but so beautifully decorated. And just walls and walls of dresses. It was a bit overwhelming really. Trying on actual wedding dresses. But it really made it sink in.

I ended up spending way more money than I thought I was going to, but I got a Maggie Sottero gown. It had a mermaid silhouette, was strapless, and had this gorgeous beading all around the bodice. The veil also had the same beading around the edge. And as I stood there, behind the little curtain, staring at myself in the mirror before revealing myself to my friends, I just had this moment of clarity—of realization. Knowing that me and Ruari were going to be together forever.

I never had any doubts about marrying him. None at all. I knew he was my soulmate. My one true love. I'd never been so certain about anything before.

And that kind of brings me onto the next thing I wanted to tell you. Well, not you specifically, Adelaide—because this could feel a bit awkward, but telling the world I guess. And that is kids. Let me just find my notes. [*Sounds of papers shuffling*] So, Ruari and I wanted kids—I mean, we'd discussed it before. We'd both said we wanted them and we'd assumed that with us being asexual that we'd adopt. But it was shortly after I'd tried on wedding dresses—and bought mine—that I was aware of a change within me. Not to say that I was becoming allosexual or anything, because I wasn't, but I felt a different... feeling. A feeling I'd not had before.

The feeling of wanting a baby with him. We'd hug and my ovaries would ache. We'd be sitting on the sofa, watching MasterChef or The Traitors and I'd look across at him and my arms would just ache. I wanted a baby. I wanted his baby.

I imagined it all the time—it's strange how quickly I became obsessed with it, and maybe it was all the wedding planning. Imagining our lives together. I wanted a little boy and a little girl, and I wanted them to look like us. Or rather, to look like him. Yeah, that was it. I didn't really mind if they looked like me or not—because I'd know they were mine. I'd know.

But I also found myself wanting to be pregnant, and this was something that I never really thought I'd want. Before, when I'd see heavily pregnant women, I'd always feel a little queasy. Uncomfortable.

But now I was imagining what it would feel like. To have a baby—his baby—growing inside me.

He was surprised when I told him this—or maybe he wasn't. I'm not sure. It was sometimes hard to read him. But we decided we'd go for IVF. This seemed like the easiest option for us. Our asexuality didn't mean we'd get it free, not like we would if we were a lesbian couple, on the NHS, but we had savings. And we talked nonstop about our baby.

"Maybe we'll have one within the first year of our marriage," he said, and I agreed, and we talked about it as if it was a given.

We planned out the whole of 2018. I had a contract for more books, and so for me it would be writing and the baby. We even picked out names.

But then the bad luck started.

Ruari's mother died very suddenly two months before the wedding. It was an overdose.

Ruari and I were in our flat. It was a cold, chilly morning, especially for May, and we were still in bed. A weekend, so we didn't feel particularly lazy about having a lie-in—because that was one thing Ruari really hated feeling. Lazy.

The heating wasn't yet on. We had it on this timer, but the timer was a bit faulty. It didn't always work when it was supposed to, so the air was cold, and I think just neither of us wanted to get up. He was playing a game on his phone, wrapped up in the duvet, and I was sort of half-asleep, imagining our kids and how perfect it would be when we were married. And then the doorbell rang. We had one of those super loud bells. You know the type for the elderly, where it's like amplified and has a speaker? Yeah, well, they're loud, aren't they? And so we both jumped when the bell rang because the speaker was in the landing area at the top of our stairs.

Ruari bolted out of bed. His side was by the window, so he peeked through the curtain.

"Shit," he said. "Police."

There were two of them. Officers in uniform. We grabbed dressing gowns to cover our pajamas—and went to let them in.

I had this weird sense of déjà vu from that dream I told you about, you know, where police are telling me something has happened to Ruari, and I remember feeling confused at first, because here they were with their somber faces, yet Ruari was fine. He was there, next to me, alive and well.

The officers sat us down. I can't remember their names, though they introduced themselves. I can't even remember what their words were. But Portia was dead.

There was fire in Ruari's eyes at first, rather than shock or grief or anything else I'd expected. "She's done this to spite us," he said, because his mother hadn't wanted us to get married. She didn't really like me—but I think it was more that she'd never have liked anyone Ruari wanted to be with.

And she hadn't liked when we'd moved in together. Mainly because it meant he wasn't injecting as much money into her household, keeping her drug habits afloat. They'd had a lot of arguments since he'd moved out, and she'd already told us somewhat gleefully that attending our wedding would be the last thing she'd ever want to do. "Even after taking out the bins and climbing inside the wheelie one and getting chucked into the garbage and ripped to shreds." Those were her exact words. I don't know how I remember that, but I do.

Ruari had pretended he didn't care. He'd told me it didn't matter, but I'd known it had hurt him, despite what he kept insisting.

But with the police in the room, Ruari just kept shaking his head and letting out this small laugh. The officers then began speaking more to me, directing all their questions and whatever else they had to say to me, rather than him, just letting him pace the room, muttering about her.

Then they left.

"Hey," I said to Ruari, my voice low. I took him in my arms, and as soon as I touched him, I felt the tension leave his body. It just melted away, and he sort of fell against me. There was this really long, low-pitched sound emitting from his chest, like a groan, but so much more.

He cried then, even though he was still muttering at the same time, about how she'd just had to do this. Had to try and ruin it for us.

[*She clears her throat*] He was determined that we'd still get married though. He said that we couldn't let it stop us. I was all set to postpone it, but he, well, he insisted.

I can't tell you just how nervous I was for our wedding ceremony. I mean, I was absolutely petrified— not that I thought Ruari would jilt me or something, just that I'd faint while we were exchanging vows. This wasn't helped by the fact that I'd been watching a lot of those 'wedding fails' reels on Instagram. You know the kind, where the bride or groom faints and 'ruins' the wedding, causing utter commotion.

I knew I shouldn't have been watching them, because they were just making me more anxious. But I couldn't stop.

The morning of the wedding was actually nice weather for a change. Like, really nice. I'd been worried it would rain—that it would rain really heavily and we'd all be soaked, but at five in the morning, as me and Julia and Hana met in the dressing room at the hotel, wide-awake despite the time, we looked out the window into the early dawn and saw warmth and stillness. A slight mist hung in the Dartmoor valleys that we could see from the sash window, and it actually looked like it was going to be an amazing day.

"Good vibes," Hana said, smiling.

Then it was a whirl of getting ready. The hairdresser and makeup artist took over the tables, my mother arrived with her nail-painting kit (we'd gone for soft pinks for me and the bridesmaids, and a soft peach for my mum), and someone soon connected their iPhone to speakers, blasting out music that I was sure was going to waken many of the guests. But of course, I was the bride, this was my wedding, and so no one said a thing.

Matilda arrived about an hour later, fresh-faced and a tad sweaty. She'd been cutting it fine with her flight getting in, but she also had some pretty expensive camera equipment with her that she'd borrowed from a mate. She was designated photographer, and it was fun, posing as we got ready, pulling silly faces, pouting into the lens.

"And let's get one with Julia putting your shoe on," Matilda said.

I'd just been crammed into my dress—that was what it felt like, cramming, because the corset had been laced up oh so tightly—and was currently sitting on the hairdresser's chair while she fussed with my locks. No sooner had Matilda spoken, when Julia seemed to materialize in front of me, with my heels in her hands.

Mum and I had chosen my heels two weeks ago, when we'd gone for my final dress fitting. They were a soft satin, but provided a lot of stability, the heel being pretty chunky. Now, Julia and I posed, like I was Cinderella seeing if the glass slipper fit.

And it did.

"Pull the skirt of your dress up just a little," Matilda advised me. "Show a little of your leg—and lift that leg up a bit too, so your muscle's not been squashed against the chair leg. We want to see the shape."

I felt so awkward posing for photos—but Matilda was right. The photos do make me look good. Not that I can really look at them much.

Once we were all ready, we headed off to the ceremony venue as a group. And it was just... I just remember it being so perfect. I'd never seen Ruari looking so handsome. Mum walked me down the aisle, and Ruari was just there, smiling so wide, with tears in his eyes. He was wearing this really nice dark blue suit that just brought out the color of his eyes more.

As I've already said, I was so nervous about the ceremony, about fainting in it or being sick, but it actually went really quickly. We said our vows, and I don't really remember many specifics, other than how warm Ruari's hand felt when he put the ring on my finger. The wedding ring! We were married.

We posed for more photos—like, proper ones, by a river, with Ruari's beloved Dartmoor as a backdrop— and then we had the reception. Julia, Hana, and Mum had done all the decorating for the room, and they'd put sunflowers and daisies, my favorite flowers, everywhere. It was so artfully done, so artistic.

Everyone was there, and I'd been worried that it might draw attention to the absence of Ruari's own mother, but he didn't mention her at all and he never seemed sad. He was the life and soul of the party that day, and well, he did get quite drunk. But who doesn't on their wedding day?

I don't usually drink alcohol, but even I had quite a few. I had this warm feeling filling my body, and it was like the ambience of the party was just carrying me around. Waiters and waitresses served finger food before the wedding breakfast, which we had quite late in the day. There were speeches there too, mainly from Mum and also Ruari's uncle. His dad was back in prison so he wasn't there. But Ruari's uncle—Portia's brother—was actually pretty cool. Not what I was expecting at all. He had this huge pink mohawk, and his suit was like this shimmery peachy color. He fitted into the wedding party really well with those colors.

So, the day went well. And Ruari and I headed off on our honeymoon the next morning, thinking we had the whole of our lives ahead of us.

The horror was only just about to begin.

And now this seems to be a good place to talk with my mother, right? And, Adelaide, you're going to like this, because I'm actually going to step out of the studio here and give you the floor. But be careful to stick to just the topics I want asked here, yeah?

On Monday, you'll get your say.

Adelaide James: Well, Mrs. Taylor, this feels odd, does it not?

Margaret Taylor: You're lucky I'm a restrained woman. Because you deserve to rot for what you've done to my daughter.

Adelaide James: [*She laughs*] Perhaps you should be careful what you say, given this is being recorded.

Margaret Taylor: I'm not a lawyer anymore, so I can say what I want.

Adelaide James: Anyway, I've got Summer's topics here. So, please, tell us about your daughter.

Margaret Taylor: She's my youngest. She's always been a bonnie little thing. Determined, headstrong when she wants to be, but so, so kind. My Summer, she'd never hurt a fly. She's always only wanted what's best for people. Always looking out for others. That's why it's so unfair what's been done to her. What those reporters and tabloids have done.

Adelaide James: Some would argue that reporters are the purest. We set the record straight. But anyway, what do you want the world to know about Summer?

Margaret Taylor: I want you all to know that she is vulnerable. She may be an amazing writer and she may be famous right now, but that doesn't mean she's invincible, unbreakable. Because my daughter has broken before—in all of this. And I do not want to be picking up the pieces again. People seem determined to give her a trial by media, even when she's never been legally accused of doing anything wrong. And that's not fair. It's things like this, things that happen to innocent people, that lead to loss. Loss of lives, and I am begging you, that if you're one of those people who's read the paper and sent Summer a message on social media, accusing her, threatening her, that you stop.

You stop and you think about what you're doing.

Because if you don't. If you continue, there will be blood on your hands.

And that is as much as I am willing to say. I am going to find my daughter now.

Day Two
Monday July 22nd, 2024

Summer Taylor-Braddon: So, Adelaide, here's how this is going to work today. I'm going to talk first. And I'm also going to introduce a couple of your most famous articles. You'll then have your chance to respond—and I gather that you've invited the first of your guests to the studio, for later today?

Adelaide James: I have, yes. And you may be sitting there all smug now, but you won't by the time I've finished with you.

Summer Taylor-Braddon: If you say so. Now, let's get back to the truth, shall we?

For a long time, Ruari and I had not been able to agree on where we were going to go for our honeymoon. We both loved natural places, and we wanted to explore somewhere we'd never been before, but there were just so many amazing places. That was our problem.

Eventually, we agreed to do a sort of tour of some of Indonesia's islands. We were starting with Sumatra, then we'd go to Bali, then Lombok.

We got the train to London Heathrow Airport and then flew from London to Kualanamu International Airport in Medan. The whole flight took something like sixteen hours, and had one stop, and to be honest, we were both grouchy when we landed because we just hadn't been able to sleep on the plane. I can't even remember what time it was there when we arrived, but we were bone-tired and as soon as we got to the hotel, we just slept.

The next day though, we were able to explore Medan. So, it's the largest city in the world's sixth largest island. That's what Ruari kept telling me. He'd looked up loads of facts about the places we were visiting, and I never checked any of them, but they sounded right.

It was kind of overcast, when we were exploring Medan. We visited palaces, mosques, museums, but it was the more everyday life that I really liked looking at. Getting a sense of how the people *live*. Don't get me wrong, the Maimun palace was amazing. It was built by—hold on, I've got my notes here. Yes, built by Sultan Ma'mun Al Rashid Perkasa Alamsyah from

1887 to 1891. The palace has thirty rooms, and the interior is this combination of design that reflected Malay culture heritage, and Islamic architecture. There is Indian architecture too, inside, and the furniture and fittings are Spanish and Italian. So, there was this real sense of amalgamation. Vibrancy. And it was kind of overwhelming—and so different to what we're used to in the West. But the bit that I found most interesting about that palace was walking around the gardens outside. It was extravagant, nicely designed—like, really nice—coconuts on trees, that sort of thing, but behind the palace, someone had set out a clothes horse. Laundry was just drying there. And I really liked that. The juxtaposition.

I liked the stalls in the city, too. People selling trinkets and ornaments, clothes, a whole array of fabrics that were just so vibrant you couldn't look away. The people were friendly too—especially when they found out we were English. Complete strangers would wave to us as we walked around outside the palaces, children asking our names, saying hello, and they were so excited when we spoke with them.

It was hot there too. I'm used to Devon where the hottest we get is probably 25 degrees Celsius most years. But there it was in the early thirties pretty much every day. It was humid too. Muggy.

We stayed in Medan for two days, I think it was, then we were off to Bali.

Bali was also very hot. Very humid, too. We were visiting a lot of temples there, starting off in Manukaya, which is this village. There's a mountain spring there. A holy mountain spring. Ruari had been reading about it in a guidebook he'd bought. It was so… tranquil. We did a lot of walking there, really taking in nature—and it was so beautiful. But hot. Each day, I was soaked in sweat, and I hadn't put on enough sun cream one day, because my skin was on fire afterward. I could hardly wear clothes at one point. It was *that* painful.

We also went to the Sacred Monkey Sanctuary too, which had this temple complex inside which was just amazing. And the monkeys! So, one grabbed Ruari's phone from him. The cheeky thing ran off with it, and Ruari went tearing after it, and I could not stop laughing—like, tears running down my face, can't breathe because I'm laughing so much. We never got it back, his phone.

We had a day trip too to one of the nearby smaller islands, Nusa Penida. A day trip from Bali. And we took so many photos, and Ruari was—he just really lit up. He's always liked rugged, natural places, and we found so many of them, but they were just so different to anything we'd experienced.

Then we went to Lombok. [*She takes a deep breath*] We were traveling around there too, and well, I honestly don't really remember much from before… before it happened. It's strange, too, because my brain has just wiped out a lot of the specifics, the details. Like, place names. Where we were staying, what we saw, where we went. A lot of people have said that that's 'convenient,' like it's proof I did something bad—you'd know all about the things people are saying.

But I didn't. I didn't do anything bad or wrong.

Ruari and I were at the beach. We were together, even though people like you seem to think I was way inland and he wasn't. But that's not true. We were both on the beach.

We were holding hands. I had this new beach dress on—mainly because it was a really floaty material, and it covered my burnt shoulders and didn't cling too much down my back either. My skin was still super bad from the sun, and though it hurt having any fabric against my body, it was the lesser of two evils.

Ruari was wearing his old swimming trunks. He had sunglasses on the top of his head, even though it was really bright. I was wearing mine. We were walking along, hand in hand. The sand was warm— and the sand was really white too, but closer to the water it had this pink tinge. I remember being just in awe at the colors—that's one thing I do remember really well. The sea was so vivid, so blue. Like turquoise-blue. So clear. And the waves lapping in gave this white plume-effect. It was like being in a painting.

I think I was carrying my shoes. Sandals. Yes, because I dropped one and had to pick it up, and Ruari made a joke about it. I can't remember what, but it was funny.

We were still laughing about it, maybe ten minutes later.

And I said to Ruari, "I can't wait to spend forever with you."

And he smiled as he turned to face me. We stopped. I looked right into his eyes, and he brought his free hand up—we were still holding hands—and he touched my face, and he said, "Forever is now."

He had a bit of sand in his hair, and he looked truly happy—properly happy.

We kissed.

I tasted the salt on his lips, and there was something about him that was so… magnetic. I didn't want to let him go. Our arms were around each other—I guess I'd dropped my sandals again—and… and he was being careful where he put his hands, what with my sunburn, only it was like I couldn't feel it.

Even though there were other people on the beach, right then, in that moment, there was only him and me. The two of us.

My heart just surged with my love for him. I was so overwhelmed by it, and being with him, embracing him like this, kissing, it just felt *right*.

Then something rumbled, and the beach just shook. Really badly. We both fell. Something hit the back of my head—his elbow, maybe, I don't know. But then people were shouting. The locals, they were all running about—and the land was still shaking. And there was this deep rumbling sound that just drilled right through me. The tourists weren't running, trying to move. They were screaming, panicking now, but I remember looking back up, at where there were like huts. Well, shops—that's what they were. Like, open-fronted, with colorful, hand-painted signs saying that Indonesian food was available there. Or cold drinks. And some had clothing, all hanging down, almost like walls of the shops—because some of these huts were just like frames, really. So the things they were selling kind of made up the walls. Like the bags! I remember the bags. Really beautiful ones, all different colors and patterns— and they were shaking so much. Falling down.

I was looking to see how the locals were reacting, because something told me this was important.

A huge roaring sound filled the air—and every hair on the back of my neck stood up. I remember inhaling sharply, feeling my chest expand, but when I tried to speak, no sound came out.

But I knew what it was, just instantly. Just like that.

I looked out at the sea, and the water was drawing backward. Away from the shore. Like this huge hand had just pulled it all back. It was this really low tide, all of a sudden. You could see the ocean floor. I remember the fish. Actual fish—suddenly flopping about. And the reefs—the textures.

I couldn't look away. There were rushing sounds in my ears, like the pounding of my own blood, as I stared. And it felt like an eternity, looking out, at the ocean floor.

Then there was…

[Silence for five seconds]

Summer Taylor-Braddon: A tsunami was coming. That was what it was. The locals were all moving inland, like, higher up. They were abandoning the wares they were selling, everything. Just moving. And shouting at the tourists, too.

I didn't know how long we had. But then the tourists—everyone on the beach was moving now as well. There was a family in front of us and they had five small children, and I remember the dad was just trying to grab all of them. Literally, all of them, in his arms.

I hadn't realized just how many people were around, until then. And… and Ruari and I got separated. It was… I was shouting for him, trying to see him. Like, doing everything I could, but everyone was panicking. I sort of got swept up in this crowd, and all I can really remember is this roaring in the air. Before the water hit. It was like thunder. And there was a really loud boom.

Then a huge wall of water hit us. It was fast. Really fast. And I could see things in the water—like arms, legs, fish. A deck chair or something hit me, in the water—not hard or anything, but it hurt. My arm. And the force of the water, it carried me.

Next thing I remember I was farther up the shore—farther than I'd realized, I think—and there were people everywhere around me. Soaked, drenched. Um, some were injured. Everyone was still trying to move. Screaming. There was lots of screaming.

I was looking for Ruari, and I was trying to go back, but someone grabbed my arm, pulled me the other way. There was this tide of people then—tide's probably not the best word to use here. Sorry. But we were all moving. There was a child next to me, injured, crying, and I picked her up. She clung to me, screaming in another language. Spanish, maybe.

I was looking for Ruari, but I assumed that he'd be in the crowd too. I thought everyone was okay.

More water came. Another wave. This was maybe thirty minutes later. That wave was worse. Bigger.

Stronger. We were on higher ground then, but it still reached us. It was just this constant battle of trying to move, trying to get away. Choking on the water. And that's when I saw what I think was my first body.

I… I didn't get a clear look at it, mind. The person just sort of floated past me, carried by the water. I was clinging to a palm tree at that point, and I just thought something like, *Oh, they're dead.*

It was strange. Because I felt calm. It wasn't until later that…

There were a series of waves. I knew tsunamis come in waves.

All I remember, after, super clearly, is the visuals. Everything was broken. And everything just kind of looked the same color. All this… rubble, I guess you'd call it. It was like this gray-brown. Everything. Broken wood—like, whole houses. Just… collapsed. Either the earthquake or the tsunami. But the water had moved everything, carried it around.

When… when the water receded, it was hard to actually comprehend the whole level of damage. Like, everything was gone.

And people were missing.

People were dead.

I was searching for Ruari.

I… I couldn't find him.

I didn't find him.

And I…

We're going to take a break now.

———————————————

Summer Taylor-Braddon: I had known at twenty-two that I couldn't live without Ruari. He was my world, and I was his. I'd spin out of control without him, with no one to orbit. We were… well, we were closer than I ever thought two people could be. It's a cliché to say that we share the same soul, but that's truly how I felt.

How I still feel.

Everyone was saying he was dead. So many people were—that was the fact of it.

I was looking and looking for him. I joined search parties. We'd find people alive, but mostly we were finding them dead.

You also couldn't really get to Lombok easily, after all the damage. Like, you just couldn't. We needed a lot of help, but it took a while for others to arrive, like from other countries. The hospitals were overrun with, well, people needing help. I wasn't really injured at all, so I didn't go to one, but they were amazing. Just the way all these Indonesian people pulled together.

I stayed there, in Lombok, a long time. There were parts of the island that were okay. Just small pockets.

Everyone was sort of being housed there. Like, hundreds of people in one building. It was a school, I think. Where I ended up sleeping. We had blankets on the floor. We were going out every day to search.

One morning before it was properly light, I got up early and left the school. There was a faint, lingering warmth to the air that managed to penetrate through my thin clothes and keep me warm, though I barely felt it. That was the thing—even though it was hot, suddenly I was cold all the time. Even in the day.

But that morning, I just needed to walk. Walk and walk and keep walking.

Every day, bodies were being recovered. The list of the dead was growing, but also the list of the missing was too. Ruari was on that list, and as time went on, more and more people were also found to be missing. There was just this whole heap of names, so many lives, and I remember thinking how selfish it was to want Ruari back, to beg God for his safe return, when I wasn't also begging for the other people to be returned, safe.

Ruari was all I could focus on.

I fell to my knees, and it felt like a chasm had opened inside my chest. A huge, gaping chasm.

Ruari was dead—I was convinced of it. truly.

I could not live without him.

I… I couldn't.

I stared down at the sea. Still dark and murky, debris floating around it, parts of buildings and furniture just floating. And I wondered, really wondered what it would be like to be inside that water. That darkness. To be hit by an armchair or a TV. To be ensnared in wires or vines or seaweed, to be held down.

I wondered if that was what Ruari had faced. If he'd been scared as the sea drowned him.

And I knew his body was most likely in there. This huge gothic monster that was a mortuary for so many.

I stared at the water—that was where my love was.

Where my life was.

I walked slowly. I couldn't hear anything but rushing sounds in my ears, like there was already water inside me. Yes—there was. That was what had been weighing me down ever since this all happened.

That's why I'd felt like I wasn't really here. Like this was happening to someone else.

Like this couldn't actually be my life.

Because my life was underwater, and that's where I was supposed to be. That's where I was.

I'd defied some law of physics, able to be in both places at once—underwater and on land. That's why I was so exhausted, because half of me was already in the dark depths. And I needed to reunite the two halves of my body. Then everything would be okay.

I was so confident of this, and as the cold water lapped my feet, as it got higher and higher up my legs, until I was waist-deep, I felt a sense of peace spreading over me.

This was what was supposed to happen.

"Everything will be okay," I said. My voice didn't sound like mine—that's one thing that really struck me at the time. Sort of jolted me out of the state I was in. Only for a few seconds. But I remember it, the sudden awareness of what I was doing, how that hit me.

How the next wave washed it away and I walked deeper into the sea.

I didn't drown. Obviously. You know that.

Two men pulled me out. My head hadn't been underwater for long. Seconds, maybe. They were local fishermen, and they'd been watching me.

I was sent to a hospital, but I didn't really need to go there. I wasn't drowning. I hadn't been drowning. I just stared at the neon lights and listened to the shouts and words of everyone around me, most of which I couldn't understand.

"We need to get you back home," Mum said to me, on the phone. I'm sure she must've said some other things too. I wanted her here, I wanted her sitting tenderly at my bedside as I waited for my blood results to come back—blood tests that I didn't even need. But Mum's words are the only ones I recall filling the room.

"I can't go back." I shook my head, clinging to the phone. I can't remember whose phone it was, but someone leant it to me. I'd spoken to Mum before that day. Called her, I think, maybe the evening that the tsunami hit. She knew I was okay. But she knew I hadn't found Ruari. "I can't leave him," I told her.

"Ruari's…" She didn't finish her sentence. She didn't have to.

"I can't leave him," I repeated, my voice steely.

"I can't lose you," was all she said, some minutes later, and I remember imagining that she was holding my hand, just like she used to when I was four years old.

Finally, I cried.

[Silence for three seconds]

Summer Taylor-Braddon: So, the problem with all this was that *Swept Away*, my first novel, was about a couple who get separated by a tsunami. It wasn't Indonesia, but that didn't matter. The love interest— the man—died in my book, and now my life was following the script I'd written.

That book was the fourth I wrote but the first to have sold to a publisher, but it hadn't sold well. It had underperformed and I had no chance of earning out on this one. That means paying back the publisher the amount they've already given you in the advance. So, if they gave you £5,000 upfront when you got the deal, then you don't get royalties until they've made that money back. So it was kind of lucky, I guess, that I'd actually signed another deal before *Swept Away* did so badly—initially anyway.

And this book was a flop, despite all the marketing that the publisher did.

But the media picked up on that. Like, the press found out that I was there. They were suddenly touting me as one of the UK's best writers, which was weird. Really weird. But it made people pay attention. And I thought it would be good because then more people would be looking for Ruari.

Or rather, for his body.

There weren't, uh… There were a lot of people dead, and a lot of people missing.

But yeah, I think we got to when Mum was helping me on the phone, right after Ruari disappeared. And… and it is difficult to talk about. I mean, I did fly home later, without him. It was October 2017, then. So, I'd stayed for three months—longer than we could've afforded really—but I had to fly home. I got a boat to Bali, I think, and I flew from there.

On the plane, I took sleeping pills. I don't know if that was a good idea or not, but it was the only way I'd be able to get through the journey, if I was out of it. Because just boarding the plane had me feeling so guilty. Like I'd just given up on Ruari. Like I was turning my back on him.

I remember the dream I had though, that pill-induced dream. I actually wrote it down, and I used it as the basis for a scene in one of my books, later on.

I can't feel anything, apart from the thing inside me.

I think it's a baby. Everyone tells me it's a baby. But it doesn't feel like a baby to me. It feels like something else. This… this swirling. This creature inside, and soon, I know, it's going to tear its way out of me, like a scene from Alien.

I don't want to be ripped apart.

But here I am, lying on a trolley. My belly is a mountain of possibility—and of fear—rising up in front of me. I cannot see my feet, and I cannot feel my legs.

All I can feel is the thing that everyone tells me is a baby.

Summer Taylor-Braddon: So, that's the scene. And in that dream I had, I was pregnant. I was pregnant with Ruari's baby, but it didn't feel like a baby. It felt like something else—something unknown. And it terrified me, that I would have this unknown thing inside me, heading into this unknown life, without Ruari.

None of this ever stops resonating with me. It's always here, in my heart. This whole thing, it's always a nightmare that I can't escape from.

And now let's have one of your wonderful articles, Adelaide.

STONE COLD KILLER OR STONE COLD PLOTTER? THE TRUTH ON SUMMER TAYLOR-BRADDON IS FINALLY HERE

By Adelaide James

Over the last few days, the nation has been gripped with a tale that seems far stranger than fiction itself. Bestselling crime writer Summer Taylor-Braddon finally tied the knot with childhood sweetheart Ruari Braddon—the very man who recently shot to fame on YouTube for his videos on Dartmoor Archaeology—and yet disaster struck upon their honeymoon.

The two lovers were honeymooning on Lombok, and then of course, the devastating tsunami struck. Taylor-Braddon was able to get herself to safety very quickly—something that makes sense, given their hotel wasn't anywhere near the affected area—yet curiously Ruari Braddon was later reported missing.

Now, there are several things about this that simply do not add up. Firstly, the missing man's phone was at the hotel. As were his shoes and all of the clothes that he was said to have taken with him. His wallet and all personal possessions were also there. Therefore, why was Ruari Braddon out and about, seemingly with nothing on, with no phone or wallet? The only thing I can believe for sure he had on was his wedding ring. And why was he so far away from his new wife?

The location that Summer Taylor-Braddon reports that she was when the tsunami struck was a good hour's car-ride away from her new husband. Why was he down on the coast, again, seemingly naked, and why was she not?

Of course, we cannot speculate that Summer knew the tsunami was about to happen, can we?

Well, as it happens, perhaps we could. Early 2017 saw the publication of Taylor-Braddon's first novel, *Swept Away*. It is a love story in which the main couple get separated, you guessed it, by a tsunami. In blog posts published around that time, Taylor-Braddon freely admits that she did a lot of research on how to spot when a tsunami is coming and the warning signs you get right before they strike. Therefore, I propose it is possible that Taylor-Braddon realized what was going to happen.

And that leads me to my next point: she purposefully asked her new husband to get swept away—or to at least appear like he has been. To go 'missing'. Here, I have two theories. One, is that she asked him to hide, so she could publicize his disappearance. I spoke to her publisher recently and a marketing consultant there told me that sales of *Swept Away,* were down. This would seem like the perfect opportunity to increase her publicity, would it not? Real life playing out exactly the way she had written it? Is Taylor-Braddon actually psychic? Or is this all a scam?

Or we have my other theory: Taylor-Braddon is a killer.

It is strange, is it not, that all of Ruari Braddon's belongings were in his hotel? Even his swimming trunks. And we know that Taylor-Braddon has a dark mind. Her second and third novels proved that, for they followed a serial killer as she went on a rampage, killing so many people, yet she was never caught. She was able to outwit everyone.

Things weren't always rosy between Taylor-Braddon and her new husband. While they had been childhood sweethearts, a source close to Taylor-Braddon told me they'd have plenty of arguments, particularly over Braddon's fondness of a tipple. Or perhaps, more than a tipple. 'It wasn't uncommon for him to drink eight pints a day,' my source told me.

And Taylor-Braddon didn't like this.

It's a common known thing, that people drink on honeymoon, and what if things got just a bit out of hand between this couple?

What if Taylor-Braddon killed her new husband in a moment of cold, calculated murder? Her internet search history is certainly questionable, and what better cover is there for that than saying that you're just a crime writer?

So, Taylor-Braddon was left with a body. A body to hide. Something she would appear an expert at. And then the tsunami struck. She could so easily have dumped the body in the hours before, ready to be swept away, while she went to higher ground, ready to play the hysterical wife who can't find her husband.

One thing is for sure: Summer Taylor-Braddon is a skilled writer, and I think she's pulled the wool over all of our eyes.

Summer Taylor-Braddon: We were warned that our situation—Ruari's disappearance—would be all over the British media. Not just when I arrived back, but that vultures like you had already been talking about it. And I was naive, I thought that it could only help. The publicity. I just wanted to find Ruari. That was all I wanted. I'd have done anything—and I thought the more people who knew, the better.

But it didn't take them long, really.

I remember the first time I saw you, Adelaide. You knocked on our front door. I was back in Devon then. You said that she'd traveled a long way to see me.

Adelaide James: I had.

Summer Taylor-Braddon: I thought you were nice—I didn't realize then that you'd already published that piece about me.

But you published another, didn't you? Two days later.

I still can't believe it—how anyone could've thought that I had killed Ruari and let the tsunami take the blame. You really went for that in your second article, lifting passages from the novels I'd written and showing how apparently it was proof of what I'd done. You made such a big thing too, out of me needing publicity because my book sales had dropped.

I'd actually signed a new deal just before *Swept Away* released—January 2017. A lot happened that month, didn't it? It had been a moderate advance with the new deal, but I remember my agent saying to me, amid all this happening in the summer, that she was really going to push for a six-figure advance for my next one. But I couldn't even imagine myself writing again, not with all this going on. Yet it was this that was making my books sell more. Everyone was talking about me.

There was a whole new group of readers I got—they all came flooding in, wanting to read my murder mysteries and psychological thrillers to see if I could've done this. They came up with all sorts of ridiculous theories. Painted me as a killer. There were whole online forums dedicated to the discussion of this.

And, well, every journalist on the planet seemed to run with that.

Mum's house was egged. Threats came in—not the death threats then. I mean, there were some of them online, the police told us, but we had actual threats arriving in the post to us. And people outside.

We stayed in a hotel for a bit, in Paris. It felt weird, flying off again with Mum, but Matilda had a shoot there, and we joined her. It was only a few hours though before our location was published and cameras were flashing outside the hotel windows.

I was in tears. Mum was in tears. Even Mattie was.

It all caught fire, you know? This small thing that you had said—had written—it blew up from there. The papers said I was guilty, had fled the country, but that French officials didn't want me there. That was apparently why I returned to the UK. Not because I live there. Not because our location had been compromised.

And it was all because of you, Adelaide James. You turned it into a witch hunt. A proper witch hunt. You'll have seen the reports about the injuries I got, right?

All I'd tried to do was go down to the Co-op. We'd run out of milk. And bread. Pretty much everything. Mum had put an online order with Morrisons in, but the driver hadn't been able to get to our house with all the paparazzi and reporters outside. I don't know if he'd tried to deliver it to us and found he couldn't, or if he'd just turned straight around and left.

But he wasn't coming.

Mum was sobbing by then. She looked pretty sick, getting iller each day. Her kidneys—though we didn't know she'd got kidney disease then—but also the stress.

"Don't worry," I told her. "I'll get the shopping tonight."

"You can't go out there!"

But I could. And I would. I told her I'd wait until it was dark, then sneak out the back. I had one of Ruari's big hoodies and I'd wear that. I did wear that. Put my hair under a baseball cap—I think that was Ashley's.

He'd left it behind, years ago. Not sure why I still had it, but I tucked my hair into it. Wore dark glasses, even though it was nighttime when I went out.

And it worked. I remember just walking down Station Road, and no one really paid attention to me. Of course, not many people were about. It was what, nine? Maybe half past. It felt like freedom.

I can't describe to you how amazing it was, how amazing it felt, just being able to do the shopping, like a normal person.

I didn't even see the person. Or the bottle of wine in their hand. Not until it was too late.

Six hours later, medics were still picking glass out of my scalp.

Adelaide James: You're good at painting yourself as the victim, aren't you?

Summer Taylor-Braddon: You know what? I'm just going to ignore you until it's actually your turn to speak. Because you may think you're the interviewer, but this is *my* project.

It didn't take long before the papers found out about Ruari's mother. What had happened. And they connected it to me. That said that I'd 'struck before'. They called me a clever killer—but not clever enough. Clever but not clever enough, and so many people believed that.

I remember reading loads of stuff posted on social media, all about me. My readers were claiming to know me. My dark fiction was a mirror to the dark interior that lurked inside my twisted mind. *It's obvious she's not right in the head,* one person wrote.

I wasn't right in the head. How could I be?

I still remember the swirling comforting hand of the sea. The relief it had promised me in a reunion with Ruari. I dreamt of it each night.

More than once, I wanted to die.

But I didn't do anything like that again. Even when I wanted to. Because for one, Mum made sure I was never on my own. She even slept in my room with me, most nights, and she always had plans for us to do in the day, things that took up literally all the time.

Not menial stuff, mind. Important stuff. We were fundraising for extra searchers to go to Indonesia to look for Ruari. We were trying to combat the media's lies, trying to talk to lawyers and solicitors and all sorts of consulates and important people.

But I couldn't go out on my own. Not to the Co-op, not anywhere.

And after a while, mum stopped trying to get me out of the house.

I just wanted to stay inside all the time. I'd watch mind-numbing TV in the gaps when there were no online meetings for me to attend. I'd do jigsaws. I'd talk to Julia and Hana, but gradually they stopped calling. Well, I mean, it's not fair to put it all on them. I never really made an effort either. And they'd done more than enough, trying to help me.

It took months for me to recover from that assault at the Co-op, physically. But it was longer than that, inside. And I've still got the scars. Ones you can see and ones you can't.

We blamed the press for it. Mum in particular blamed you, Adelaide.

"She does this with everyone she writes about," Mum told me. She'd been researching you. Looking at other people you had gone after. Some ballerina at a London school who you accused of killing her twin. Something like that. All lies.

But now you were doing it to me. And I thought that maybe when I was in hospital, recovering, that you'd have stopped. I thought you couldn't possibly do any worse.

I was wrong.

THE KILLER ON YOUR DOORSTEP

By Adelaide James

As a society, we are supposed to be against murdering one another. It's something we're not supposed to do. We're supposed to hate anyone who does, we're supposed to lock them up, right?

Wrong.

We only lock them up if they're not a beautiful white woman.

How do I know this? Well, Summer Taylor-Braddon is still out there. She's living in Okehampton. At the top of Station Road, a little bird tells me. And she's really got her life sorted now, hasn't she?

First, she planned out her murders. She even wrote about them in her novels—perhaps that was a test of sorts, to see if readers would believe it? And it gave her an excuse to research exactly how to do it, with no one suspecting.

Second, she chose a honeymoon location where earthquakes and tsunamis are relatively common.

Thirdly, she just had to wait and strike while the iron was hot. While a tsunami was forecast. She murdered her husband, and she covered it up.

And now of course she's raking in the millions from her book sales, using this all to get more publicity. She has even just signed a new book deal for three new thriller novels to release starting next year.

And I just have to ask myself, why are we so happy to let this killer walk free?

And who will she strike down next?

Anonymous commenter: She's so sick, that woman. She should be locked up.

Anonymous commenter: I can't believe she's still doing all these TV appeals, pretending to care for him. To be the doting loving wife.

Anonymous commenter: She's a killer, for sure.

Anonymous commenter: Well, what are we waiting for guys, we know where she lives now!!!

Summer Taylor-Braddon: And now, Adelaide—let's bring you into all of this now. Remember that we're only focusing so far on the events already narrated, but tell everyone why you were right to publish what you did.

Adelaide James: My job is to make sure that no wool is pulled over people's eyes. Everyone was so sure at first that you were innocent. Tragic, they called you. But you're not an innocent type of person, are you, Summer? You play the victim so well, but I can see through you. It may be that my theories were wrong— but I wasn't wrong completely, was I? We all know what you did later.

Summer Taylor-Braddon: I already said we're sticking only to events already narrated, Adelaide.

Adelaide James: Don't the public deserve to know?

Summer Taylor-Braddon: And they will know. They will—when we get to that part. You've got my outline, so you know what we're talking about when.

Adelaide James: You think you're so clever, don't you? You think that you can really script everything, don't you? Talk people around. You may be a writer, but you're not invincible. And no—don't speak. Let me talk. I've got a lot to say.

And I know you're not going to like this. Hell, you may even edit these recordings, and I know this is your project and there's nothing I can actually do about that, except try. Try and get the truth across.

I am going to bring my first guest in now. This promises to be a very interesting conversation.

Adelaide James: So, with us in the studio, we have Hector Beveridge. Welcome, Mr. Beveridge. So, Ms. Taylor-Braddon, I assume you remember who this man is?

Summer Taylor-Braddon: My primary school teacher. Year 2.

Adelaide James: Yes. [*She clears her throat*] Now, Hector, perhaps you'd like to start by telling us what Ms. Taylor-Braddon was like as a child?

Hector Beveridge: A tearaway! [*He laughs*] There were two classes per year in our school back then, and Summer was notorious. She was one of those children that today hundreds of emails would be sent about. I always taught year 2, which meant I also kept an eye on the year 1s, seeing who I'd have the following year. Summer came to my attention early on.

Adelaide James: And why might that be?

Hector Beveridge: She had a reputation. She was one of those kids who'd really test anyone she was with. You'd tell her "no" and she wouldn't just say "why" but she'd do it anyway, right after you told her not to. She always had to have her own way. She had to be the center of attention, and really, it was dangerous if she wasn't the center, because then you knew she was planning something. She'd bite other children, break their toys, and she'd scream so loudly if she wasn't getting what she wanted.

But she was also clever too. Very intelligent. Not just academically, but even when she was playing up, she'd show she was clever. She did enough to get temporarily suspended, but never excluded. When she'd come back she'd be ever so nice. Good as gold. And I'd just know that she was planning something. She was like an alarm clock ready to go off, only just when you thought the alarm would blare through the room, it wouldn't.

It was always the waiting, with Summer. Waiting to see what she was going to do next.

Adelaide James: That makes her sound like quite the difficult child?

Hector Beveridge: Difficult, yes. But she was still likable too. That was the odd thing. Usually if there was a badly behaved kid in the class, none of the other children really liked them. And although Summer had made plenty of enemies in the classroom—the kids she bit and kicked, for example—she still had a lot of friends. She was liked, and she definitely had a spark to her. I was more fond of her than I cared to admit, at the time.

I knew she'd do great things, if only she put her mind to it. That was why I was so excited to see she was making it as an author. She was putting her mind to good use. And she'd always been good at literacy.

Adelaide James: Yes, tell us more about that, Mr. Beveridge. I understand that as a child, Ms. Taylor-Braddon was quite imaginative?

Hector Beveridge: Aye, that she was.

Adelaide James: But it wasn't just in literacy and English lessons, was it? She'd—well, what other word for there is it, than *lying*?

Hector Beveridge: This was a particular concern after Christmas, when she was in my class, yes. She was… imaginative. But she was also convincing.

She told me her family had got a puppy for Christmas. She told me its name—I forget what that was now—but she gave so many details, describing it. Telling us all in the class about what the dog was like, where they took it for walks. She even brought in its lead for show-and-tell.

It was only a couple months later when I asked her mother at parents' evening how the dog was getting on. She didn't have a clue what I was talking about.

Adelaide James: So, she was lying?

Hector Beveridge: She told a lot of stories about this dog.

Adelaide James: But it wasn't just stories about the dog, was it? There were other lies.

Hector Beveridge: There were.

Adelaide James: Care to elaborate, Mr. Beveridge?

Hector Beveridge: I… Sorry, Summer, it doesn't seem right talking like this, with you in the room. And all children do lie. We encourage creativity in school, and that was what it was.

Adelaide James: Mr. Beveridge, *please*. We are here to talk about the truth. Ms. Taylor-Braddon can handle hearing the truth about herself, for she is on a quest to reveal the truth to everyone.

Hector Beveridge: She was very imaginative, even then.

Adelaide James: And what was the worst lie she told? I assume it wasn't this thing about the dog?

Hector Beveridge: It wasn't, no. [*He takes a deep breath*] She told us her sister was missing.

Adelaide James: Matilda Taylor?

Hector Beveridge: Matilda Taylor. Summer came in one morning, very upset. Tears running down her face. She couldn't be consoled. She'd already told us that her sister—I think Matilda was about seventeen then—

she'd told us Matilda was a model. We were all excited for her. Most of us at the school, teachers that is, remembered when Matilda was in our classes. And that morning Summer said that Matilda was missing. In Paris. She'd gone for a photoshoot there, and she hadn't been heard of for two days.

The thing about Summer was when she told her stories, she could be very persuasive. Given how upset she was, I had no reason to doubt her. And she was giving all these details—like the police looking for Matilda, and how officers had been round the house to talk to Summer and her mother—that I find it hard to believe a seven-year-old would know if none of it had actually happened.

I don't know why she decided to make that up. But she had the school phoning home, us offering our support to her mother. We were even thinking about a fundraiser or campaign thing that we could do to help.

Adelaide James: But none of that was true, was it?

Hector Beveridge: No, it wasn't.

Adelaide James: Thank you, Mr. Beveridge, that is all.

Adelaide James: One thing that was very interesting just now, Ms. Taylor-Braddon, was watching your body language while Mr. Beveridge was talking. You've already told us that body language is an integral part of communication, and yours was full of clues. The tense posture, the way you kept fidgeting, and you really didn't want to make eye contact with either me or Mr. Beveridge during that conversation, did you?

Summer Taylor-Braddon: I was fidgeting because I needed the toilet. That was all. And you'll find I did make eye contact.

Adelaide James: But it's never comfortable, is it? Hearing what you're really like. Listening to people tell the truth.

Oh, are you not answering that? Well, that's telling in and of itself, would you not agree?

Summer Taylor-Braddon: I can see what you're doing—because that's what you've always done. Made me out to be a liar.

Adelaide James: Oh, but Ms. Taylor-Braddon, we've just had an independent party confirm that you are a liar. He described in very convincing detail two different occasions when you lied. Do you admit those were lies you told?

Summer Taylor-Braddon: Yes, I did lie about the dog and Mattie going missing. But I was a child.

Adelaide James: Children who lie often become adults who lie.

Summer Taylor-Braddon: But they often don't.

Adelaide James: That seems a very weak argument. But perhaps you'd like to elaborate on all of this and really explain why, when you introduced yourself at the start of this project, you didn't mention any of this. Instead, you painted this image of yourself as an honest, nice girl. A girl your mother could be proud of. There was no mention of any incidents such as the ones Mr. Beveridge mentioned, and well, that just makes me question how reliable anything you tell us might be?

Summer Taylor-Braddon: I was seven years old then, as has been pointed out numerous times. Children lie, and they test adults with what they can get away with. But I grew up. I think it's telling that you haven't brought in any teachers from my secondary school. I didn't lie there. And I haven't lied since.

Adelaide James: I'm looking at you now, and you seem pretty relaxed. You're leaning back, one leg crossed over the other. You're not sweating at all. You don't look nervous now.

Summer Taylor-Braddon: Why would I be nervous? I've done nothing wrong.

Adelaide James: You know who else doesn't look nervous? A psychopath.

Summer Taylor-Braddon: Are you really saying that I'm a psychopath? [*She laughs*] Just earlier, you were saying I looked defensive, when you were talking to my teacher. Surely a psychopath wouldn't look defensive there, if they—allegedly—thought they were being caught out? Aren't they supposed to be super calm?

Adelaide James: You tell me, Ms. Taylor-Braddon. You appear to be the expert on psychopaths. But you have just brought up something interesting. That you think you are going to be caught out.

Summer Taylor-Braddon: I never said that.

Adelaide James: But I think everyone will agree that you know how to spin a story. Your success as an author is proof of that. How do we know that you're not the ultimate unreliable narrator, even now?

Summer Taylor-Braddon: Look, Adelaide, your views and mine are never going to go off hand-in-hand with each other, into the sunset, are they? I'm telling my story, and you're apparently telling yours.

Adelaide James: And now you're being condescending. That makes you seem defensive. Like you've got something to hide.

Summer Taylor-Braddon: You want to know how I feel? How I really feel? I still feel trapped, because of what you and other journalists have done to me. It's like the whole world is a prison now. I only really feel safe at home—but nowhere actually feels like home now. We've had to move so much, every time our location is published, we've moved.

My whole life has changed, and it feels like so few people understand.

I just want to escape.

Adelaide James: I guess that explains why you're writing all the time now. Why you're desperate to distract yourself. It's a great form of escape, is it not?

Summer Taylor-Braddon: The only form I've got.

Adelaide James: And were you writing, during this time that you were talking about earlier? When you returned to England, after Ruari apparently disappeared?

Summer Taylor-Braddon: No, I wasn't. It felt too indulgent to do it, even though I knew I needed to. I mean, I had books under contract. They'd sold on proposal, but I hadn't yet written them. Only had maybe three chapters of two of them done. The third was just a vague one-paragraph pitch. So I felt pressure to write. But also, I needed to for my mental health—but my mental health was always going to be shot to pieces when he wasn't there.

Adelaide James: You like playing that card don't you?

Summer Taylor-Braddon: What card?

Adelaide James: The mental health card.

Summer Taylor-Braddon: Look, the whole time I'd been having these nightmares—so many different ones too. It wasn't like it was the same one, because even that would've been better, been reassuring. A part of my subconscious would've known what was coming and I'd have been able to prepare.

But these nightmares were all so, so different. The unpredictability was the worst.

Mum wanted me to see a therapist. Deep down, even I wanted me to see a therapist. But I couldn't face it.

Adelaide James: Of course you couldn't, because they'd know that you were lying about it. Not really having any of these "nightmares". That it was all a lie, to get sympathy.

Summer Taylor-Braddon: I couldn't leave the house. I was terrified. We'd had people trying to break in at the last place—this whole group of men showing up and trying to break down the front door. They broke one of the windows too. There was broken glass everywhere, and I called the police as I locked myself in the bathroom upstairs. I was so scared, just waiting for these people to hurt me.

The police did get there in time. Arrested the men. But it didn't really stop that sort of thing from happening.

It didn't make me feel any safer.

So instead, I wrote.

Adelaide James: Oh, what a difficult time that must have been—penning your next multi-million-pound book.

Summer Taylor-Braddon: It was therapy writing, actually.

Adelaide James: Of course it was. Anything can be a therapy-thing now, right? Therapy-writing, therapy-guinea-pig, therapy-sofa. It's getting quite out of hand.

Summer Taylor-Braddon: Therapy writing is valid. It helps you take back control of your mental health. And the more I wrote about myself and the feelings and how I thought about the sea now, the more I realized this wasn't what I needed to be writing.

Writing fiction helps me process and understand myself. Writing fiction opens up a part of my soul that lets light in, that heals. And so I began writing stories again. I opened my notebook and I chose a nice pen. I scribbled words—frantically, furiously at first, until I bled over the page, raw, acrid.

Adelaide James: You like being dramatic, don't you?

Summer Taylor-Braddon: These are my words. This is my story. But after I had written for a while—yes, these *silly little therapy writings*—that night, for the first night in a long time, I didn't have a nightmare.

I dreamed instead of Ruari in a calm way. A loving way.

And when I woke up, I knew it was a sign—a sign from Heaven, I believed. He was telling me he was okay. And so long as I wrote every day, continued writing my stories and trying to look after my mental health, I'd be able to live with him in my dreams.

But it was never that simple.

That, and there were sightings of him.

Adelaide James: Ah, the famous sightings.

Summer Taylor-Braddon: There were quite a lot, weren't there? There were always going to be, with this being a high-profile disappearance. But it wasn't *just* sightings of him. Men came forward. They said they *were* Ruari. It was cruel, you know. Because I'd always really hope. I'd really believe that my Ruari was about to come home. That we'd be reunited.

And I believed it every day. The disappointment, with each one, just got worse.

Adelaide James: Of course it did.

Summer Taylor-Braddon: It really did.

Adelaide James: You knew all along what was going on. You used the world as your page, and you tried to sculpt a narrative that we'd all believe. These potential sightings were all part of your plan. You can't lie anymore, Ms. Taylor-Braddon.

Summer Taylor-Braddon: I'm not lying.

Adelaide James: You're a manipulative bitch.

Summer Taylor-Braddon: [*She takes a deep breath*] The police had to get involved in the end, given how many people were pretending to be him, like this. They issued warnings, said there'd be strict penalties. It didn't really deter people. Because those first couple of years, there were thousands of people coming forward, saying they were him.

And I wanted to ignore each new one, but still a part of me hoped.

Adelaide James: Poor little Ms. Taylor-Braddon. This just sounds like torture.

Summer Taylor-Braddon: It *was*. I even phoned the Samaritans once. I didn't tell them who I was and I couldn't really give details of what was going on—that would've made me recognizable instantly—but I just told them that I felt like I was being played with. Told them how scared I was.

It was good to talk to them, even if I couldn't go into details. It made me feel heard.

After about six months, I saw a new therapist. She suggested I try writing more therapy writings, to directly deal with my feelings over Ruari's death—that's what everyone called it. His death. Even though there was still no body.

I don't really remember what else she said beyond that.

Except that I should write about my grief. I don't know if she suggested that I write about Ruari—if maybe she meant to write our memories, or if it was what I did—writing a future for us. But I started writing. A story that began with us newly married, on our honeymoon. The bad thing still happened, but not to us—because we left Indonesia the day before it happened, in this version.

Adelaide James: So, as if you hadn't already made enough money on your books from Ruari's disappearance, you then wrote another! This time, about it! It really beggars belief.

Summer Taylor-Braddon: It was therapeutic, writing it. Us on the plane back, getting to our house. A new house that we'd just bought.

I changed our names of course, but there was no doubt in my mind that I was writing about us. And I penned this whole love story. The love story that I'd wanted. The love story that I'd thought we'd have.

Adelaide James: Whatever. Let's have a break. I need a stronger drink if I've got to listen to much more of this.

Summer Taylor-Braddon: I saw Ruari, once you know. When he was missing.

Adelaide James: Of course you did. [*She laughs*] You just can't remember all the lies you've spun, can you? Pretending he's missing, that you don't know a thing about where he is, and then you go and admit this.

Summer Taylor-Braddon: Yeah. I saw him. From my bedroom window. Just the once. It was dark, evening. The street lights were on but they were those weird bulbs. Like, yellow. Everything looked a dark yellow. Eerie. And I saw him.

He was standing directly below my window, looking up at me.

He smiled and he mouthed the words 'it'll be okay'.

And then he was gone.

Adelaide James: Okay.

Summer Taylor-Braddon: You can roll your eyes all you like at me. I'm not lying. I saw him—even though he wasn't there. And I'm not crazy, either. Well, maybe I was. Or I am. I don't know. But I took it as a sign. Another sign that everything was well, wherever he was, as well as it could possibly be. That I was doing the right thing by writing our story. And you know, when I eventually finished it, my agent loved this new book. She said it was different to my thrillers—of course it was—but she thought it would sell. I learned later it was more that she thought *anything* written under my name would sell. It didn't matter what it was.

But I didn't realize that at the time. I was so swept up in writing *The Saga of Me and Him,* the what could have beens. It was a whirlwind. The manuscript got longer and longer. Next I knew, my agent was taking it to auction.

It sold for seven figures.

Adelaide James: Seriously, drop the act, Ms. Taylor-Braddon. You knew it would sell. That's why you wrote it!

Summer Taylor-Braddon: I had more money after that, yes. Mum and I were able to get some security in. We felt a bit more protected.

Adelaide James: [*She laughs*] So, tell us the next part in your masterplan?

Summer Taylor-Braddon: The years passed, and I kept writing. I couldn't not. I had to write the three thrillers I'd been contracted for as well—I mean, these are the ones I signed the deal for in January 2017, before *Swept Away* released. The books were delayed in the end, with everything going on, but I did write them eventually. It was 2020 and 2021 when they finally released, right in the middle of lockdown. But my heart wasn't in those books. I wanted to continue writing about me and Ruari—and that was what the world wanted too.

I wrote and wrote; writing was my drug, because I was now not only living with him at night, in my dreams, but on the page, too. I was writing our story. I was keeping him alive, keeping myself alive.

The Saga of Me and Him turned into an eight-book series. The books got on several bestseller lists. *New York Times, USA Today, Sunday Times*. Each new novel centered around a new couple—a couple that had been introduced in the previous book—talking of their epic love story, but it was always me and Ruari. Always.

We went through everything together, in those books.

Adelaide James: How lovely for you.

Summer Taylor-Braddon: Only it wasn't. Publishing those books was so different. And hold on—I've got my notes here on this. On how I want to say it.

Adelaide James: And this is the woman who doesn't plan to manipulate us, ha!

Summer Taylor-Braddon: Most authors have to do a lot of events. Publishers encourage it, especially when a new book is releasing. It gets more attention on it. I'd done a few events before—signings at local bookstores, a couple of conventions, and I'd spoken on panels at CrimeFest in Bristol two years running—this was before the wedding. The honeymoon.

But when *The Saga* released, I wasn't doing events anymore. It wasn't safe. Just the thought of exposing myself to complete strangers scared me, but I also missed the interaction on a deeper level.

Before, at some of my signings, readers would tell me their favorite scenes in the books, and I always enjoyed that. But now I wasn't getting that, so I started paying more attention to the reviews. More and more, I was on Goodreads, which of course is not a place for writers at all.

But I wasn't reading everything there that was being written about my books—and of course, there were things about me. A lot of hate. But I would also find stuff that was useful to me. Literary discussions about my books, my plots. And there was one comment that really stuck with me.

The Saga was romance. That was mainly how it was being marketed. But this one person was complaining there was no spice. They wrote something like, 'Has this author ever even been laid?' and that comment really got to me.

I wondered then if they could tell I was asexual from reading my books. Because I wasn't writing about sex. I was only writing about love. Even though pretty much everyone else—it felt like—saw them as entwined. You can't have one without the other, and all that.

So, with the final Saga book, I wrote a sex scene.

I had to read a lot of them at first, and I kind of got into reading these more explicit romances. So, soon I was able to write more sexy stuff.

After all eight of the *Saga* books were out, I got a deal for a standalone romance. A Christmas romance. This was *Just in Time*, which released in September 2023. The publisher wanted a lot of sex, because sex sells. So, I wrote it.

It was easier than I thought.

One day, Hana and Julia had come over. We were hanging out in my living room—Mum was out—and Hana had the last of the *Saga* books in her hand. She opened the sex scene—she'd bookmarked it—and she asked me why I had written it.

"I really loved that these books were closed-door," she said. "That these were books you could tell your mother that you were reading, without getting embarrassed."

I told her that I'd wanted to see if I could write it: sex.

"But why wouldn't you be able to?" Julia had asked. "You and Ruari were living the greatest love story of all time."

I don't really remember a moment where I took a deep breath or anything, a moment where I knew I was about to tell them what felt like my biggest secret. It just came out, naturally. And these were my best friends, so I had no reason to think they wouldn't be supportive.

"I'm asexual," I said, and I said it so simply. Other than talking to Ruari about my sexuality, this was the first time I'd had a conversation with anyone where it was about me being asexual.

I recall that Hana just nodded. She'd already come out as a lesbian shortly after we left school, and she was pretty open to it all. But Julia just stared at me.

The thing about Julia is that she's always had this viciousness within her. She and Hana were friends from nursery. Best friends. It had been the two of them for so long, but then in year 7, I joined them. I thought that we could be an equal trio. Best friends, the three of us.

Julia didn't like me, then. She felt threatened, I can see that now. I was trying to take her best friend away, in her eyes. She didn't like that at all. But she wasn't mean to me or anything then. No, she was clever about it. She started a few rumors about me, among the other girls, and then when I'd been upset, she'd be my shoulder to cry on.

She was pretty manipulative, all things considered. Kind of like you, Adelaide.

But as we got older, we kind of came to an understanding. We became friends, more solidly, started hanging out just the two of us. It took us longer, because she was threatened by me. And because I knew she had this streak within her.

I was always nervous around her—I can see that now, looking back. Even when I thought we were close, I was guarded. I had to be.

"You're writing romance and you're *asexual*?" Julia had looked at me with contempt then. "This whole series of books is lies?"

"The series is about love," I said.

"But your love story is a lie."

"My love story is not a lie. Love and sex are different," I countered. "I've been writing about love."

She looked at me with such disgust that it made her nostrils flare. Her nose ring glinted with the movement. "Doesn't it make you feel like a fraud?"

Hana spoke up then, backing me, but I stopped listening.

I remember how sick I felt, how I couldn't wait for Julia to leave.

She did, eventually. And the next time I saw her, she acted as if nothing had happened, but I knew that she held this disgust of me.

And then a month later, you found out about me being ace. You wrote a huge article about it, calling me a fraud, didn't you?

I was convinced Julia must've leaked it. It wasn't her place, or yours, to tell the world! And I didn't want everyone knowing! I didn't want that to be used as yet another attack on me.

I was scathing, going through Julia's social media profiles, looking for anything she might've said. I couldn't see anything, and I rang her. I was so angry.

She just snapped at me, "Of course I wouldn't out you."

But someone had.

And I knew it wouldn't have been Hana.

BESTSELLING "ROMANCE" NOVELIST HAS NEVER HAD SEX!

By Adelaide James

In recent years, bestselling author Summer Taylor-Braddon has made quite the headlines. Her biggest publicity efforts of course have been the scripted disappearance of her husband Ruari Braddon on their honeymoon in Lombok. Taylor-Braddon alleges that her beloved went missing during the catastrophic tsunami that hit Indonesia's islands in July 2017, but the wool isn't as easy to pull over all our eyes.

Summer Taylor-Braddon has pulled off quite the remarkable feat. She has managed to stay out of prison, despite her criminal activities. She has even managed to write another shelf of bestsellers—all now firmly in the romance genre.

Reading *The Saga of Me and Him*—which, let's face it, is an awful name—one might think that Taylor-Braddon herself must have had the best lived love story ever. Yet a source close to the author has just revealed exclusively to me that Summer Taylor-Braddon is asexual.

This, more than anything, proves that Taylor-Braddon is a fraud and a liar. Not just in terms of what really happened to Ruari Braddon, but in her whole career as a writer. How can someone as cold and unfeeling as Taylor-Braddon write romance? Yet she had us all hooked in by her books.

A startling discovery, many of you will agree—but it has made me think more critically about Ruari Braddon's role in all of this. Previously, I wasn't too sure whether Ruari was part of Taylor-Braddon's plans willingly or not. Was he a cunning man willing to hide out for years or was he a victim, his body discarded in the ocean by Taylor-Braddon?

Now, however, I feel most sorry for Ruari Braddon, as I am sure many of you also will. With this revelation about Summer Taylor-Braddon's sexuality, we now find that Ruari Braddon was definitely a victim. A poor man trapped in a sexless and loveless marriage, where even his most basic needs were not being met.

Yet it also brings a new angle to Taylor-Braddon's story. This woman is clearly very unwell and needs psychiatric help. Not just with her compulsive lying and criminality, but she needs to see someone about her lack of sex drive. After all, that really can't be healthy, can it? And maybe this lack of sex drive is the root of all her problems.

Summer Taylor-Braddon: That was the article that really hurt me the most. The blatant acephobia in it.

Adelaide James: As a journalist, I have a duty of care to the public. I have to expose the lies and corruption in society.

Summer Taylor-Braddon: You got hate mail, after publishing that article, if I understand it rightly?

Adelaide James: I did. Many LGBTQIA+ people and activists weren't too happy with me.

Summer Taylor-Braddon: You know, that actually cheered me up a bit. Knowing that the queer community could see what a horrid person you were.

Adelaide James: I hold my hands up freely now, that publishing that article, in that way, was wrong. I admit my mistakes, unlike some people. But at the time, I did not understand asexuality. I thought it was an unnatural thing.

Summer Taylor-Braddon: And you thought I'd trapped Ruari in a sexless marriage.

Adelaide James: You had. I still stand by that now. I don't believe any of what you've said about him being asexual as well.

Summer Taylor-Braddon: Why?

Adelaide James: It's too convenient. Why not tell the world this several years ago, when your asexuality made headlines?

Summer Taylor-Braddon: Because unlike you, I have a problem with outing people. And that article you wrote, outing me, this was just a convenient way for you to try and stay relevant—attacking me and circulating a third theory about why I was the villain. Saying he'd staged his own disappearance to get away from me.

And, of course Mum found out I was ace because of you. She sat me down and asked if it was true. Her voice was so soft, and she seemed really worried.

I said, "It doesn't matter."

She said, "Did you not feel able to tell me?"

"I didn't think it was a big deal," I said, only that was a lie. All along, my asexuality had been my secret because it *was* a big deal. I was scared of ignorant and hateful reactions from people like you, Adelaide.

But Mum was supportive. She didn't understand it, but she was supportive. There for me, like always.

Adelaide James: So, I understand you never dated anyone else during this time Ruari was… away?

Summer Taylor-Braddon: No, I didn't.

A couple of times, over the next few years, Mum asked me if I wanted to talk to people online. I thought she meant more therapists, but turned out she meant dating sites.

Meet another man.

"No," I said. "You didn't. You never dated after Dad died."

"I knew that he had passed away though," she said. "It was different."

"No—you had *closure*, and still you didn't," I pointed out.

She nodded and never mentioned it again, but it really got me thinking. What if I did try and date again—not now, of course. But in the future. Ten years' time or something.

Then I felt angry, sad, guilty.

Nothing could compare to what me and Ruari had.

And Ruari, he was still out there.

[Silence for three seconds]

Summer Taylor-Braddon: I often wondered what I'd do if his body was found. It seemed unlikely now, all these years later, but I kept thinking about it, conjuring up the whole scene, scenario in my head. Coming up with dialogue and different reactions for me.

But I could never actually tell what would happen. Would I lose it completely?

Would I be compelled to drown myself?

Or would I move on with my life, having got the closure that everyone seemed to think I needed.

But the only closure I wanted was that he was still alive.

If he was dead, I knew I wouldn't be able to cope, whether I was living or not.

And it was wrong of me to imagine a life where I might meet someone else—because they wouldn't be Ruari. They wouldn't be the love of my life. And I'd always be comparing this new person to him.

That wouldn't be fair on either of us.

But then… Then we heard the news that I'd been living for, hoping for, dreaming for. I was actually recording an interview for a podcast. *Just in Time* had released the month before. I was chatting to a man called Brent, talking about Christmas cheer and trying to sound really happy, even though I had a killer headache and really bad period pains—the kind that just make it hard to sit up and think coherently. And then my phone started blowing up. So many calls— some from withheld numbers, but then after ten minutes—I was still chatting to Brent, trying to sound jolly—my mum was phoning me too.

It was 8th October 2023. Ruari Braddon, my husband, had been found.

Ruari Braddon, my husband, was alive.

Day Three
Tuesday July 23ʳᵈ, 2024

Summer Taylor-Braddon: What's your favorite flower?

Adelaide James: Sorry, what?

Summer Taylor-Braddon: Your favorite flower? Come on, you must have one.

Adelaide James: I've always liked honeysuckle, I guess.

Summer Taylor-Braddon: I've always liked daisies. There's something beautiful about them, even though they're so ordinary. So simple. Those delicate white petals, the yellow center. The reassurance of them—that if you go to any grassy space, there's a good chance you'll find them.

They're there. They're reliable.

But whenever you ask someone their favorite flower, no one ever really says the daisy. It's overlooked. People might say roses—because they're beautiful, they're works of art with the way their petals all whirl together. Or they might say lilies, with their elegance and gracefulness, the ballerinas of the flower world. Or they'll say a dahlia or a chrysanthemum or a tulip or any other number of flowers. Or they'll be like you and say honeysuckle—something sweet. Supposedly.

But I am a daisy. I feel that—have often felt that. I'm not massively beautiful or anything. People don't stop to look at me in the street when they see me because of my beauty or my body.

I am a daisy that's been magnified, made into this giant monster. People see me now, and they stop and stare, because of what's been done to me. The daisy that's been made enormous in the lab.

And I just want to go back to the grassy fields. I want to sit there with my friends, unnoticed, but constant. Reassuring.

But most of all I want Ruari, because he's my field. He's where I am at my safest.

And now he was back.

Adelaide James: Did you always plan for him to come back then, or had he just decided not to play along with your plan anymore?

Summer Taylor-Braddon: You know what, Adelaide? I'm not answering your questions just at the moment. I'm going to talk—tell my story. And then after I've talked, you'll hear from my next guests. We'll probably break that section up into several sessions, okay? You can talk afterward.

Adelaide James: Again, the interviewer normally decides how this goes.

Summer Taylor-Braddon: Again, this is my story. I'll let you know when you can speak again.

Adelaide James: I'm not one of your characters.

Summer Taylor-Braddon: But you'll do as I say—otherwise I can just find some other journalist to work with me on this.

[Summer takes a deep breath]

Summer Taylor-Braddon: *He's a bit confused.*
That's what they told me first. Some doctors at the hospital said this to me over the phone. The British consulates all repeated it. Mum said it to me too. *He's a bit confused* became this mantra that just kept following me around, as I frantically tried to pack.

We were flown out to Australia, me and Mum, because that's where he'd now turned up. No one really knows for sure how he got there. Whether he'd truly been swept in the ocean all that way, or if he'd been on a boat, a canoe.

There were so many official people about. The British consulates of several of the Australian cities and loads of police and security. There were lawyers, too, and medics.

I didn't know about Ruari's amnesia then. They didn't tell me. I don't know why. Why they thought that telling me he was a bit confused was enough.

Mum and I were in the hotel room that had been designed to be the meeting place. The reunion. Annmarie, one of the British consulates, was also here. She was sitting by the tea and coffee facilities, in her impeccable suit. A soft-gray pencil skirt and matching blazer.

Outside, the reporters were everywhere, and Annmarie was tapping away on her phone. "He's being brought around the back way," she told me, a few moments later.

I felt so, so sick. I fidgeted, couldn't decide whether I should sit on the bed or at the desk. There were two chairs at the desk, and another by the window. There was too much choice, and I was like a jack-in-the-box, constantly on the go.

Mum came to my rescue, placing her hand on my arm as I sat down for what felt like the hundredth time. "It'll be okay," she said. There were tears in her eyes. "You're getting Ruari back."

I'd not thought before how hard this must be for her. I was getting a second chance that had never been offered to her. I smiled, was about to say something, when the door opened.

The first person wasn't Ruari. It was a tall, thin Black man in a suit, and the second person wasn't him either—that was an Asian woman who was speaking on her phone. The third person was a white policeman, and then—then I saw him.

Ruari Braddon stepped hesitantly into the room, walking in a way that he'd never walked before. He'd always seemed so confident. So sure of himself, even when he was at school and shy. He had this presence. But now he walked with the air of someone much smaller, much shier. It was like his body was falling in on himself. He glanced around anxiously. His brows knitted together—and that was a familiar expression on his face. I'd seen it so many times before.

And that was enough for me.

I couldn't move fast enough. "Ruari!" My heart pounded, and I reached him. My arms sprang around him, and I held him so tight. I was shaking, trembling so hard that I was nearly falling over, but his arms fell around me, and he held me.

He didn't smell like how he used to—the shock of that really hit me, made my tears fall onto his jacket. A corduroy jacket—something that he'd never have worn. But I didn't care.

I held him and I cried, and he held me.

"Summer?"

I was vaguely aware of my mum and Annmarie talking to me, and then I felt a hand on my shoulder that wasn't Ruari's. I wanted to swat it away, but of course I didn't.

I just pulled back from Ruari enough to see his face. He had aged in the last six years. Quite a lot actually. And there was a scar on the side of his head that I figured must be from the tsunami. It was jagged and looked bumpy in texture, from the corner of his left eye, down his face. Long, meandering, like a snake.

He was sweating a bit, perspiration collecting on his brow, and he held his head at an angle.

His eyes were the same. Relief pounded through me. *His eyes were the same.*

"Who…who are you?" he asked.

I laughed—it just burst out of me, and I couldn't stop. I laughed and laughed, and during my laughter, the two of us got separated. Mum was now holding me, and I saw the worried look on her face. I heard snatches of the conversation then—from Annmarie, and the officials, and…

Ruari wasn't joking. He didn't know me. His eyes, though they were the same, they were also different. Because I fought until I was away from my mum's arms and back in front of Ruari, looking into his eyes. For the lightheadedness, for the corners of his eyes to crinkle as he smiled and yelled, "just kidding!"

But he didn't yell. He just stared at me.

There was an emptiness in those beautiful eyes of his. A lack of recognition.

Now, I'm angry about this, about not being told by the doctors, because *he's a bit confused* means he's a bit confused, not that he has no fucking memory of our life together. Of me.

I don't remember the rest of the reunion. I know that one of the reporters got it all on tape, that pretty much everyone in the UK has listened to it. It was broadcast everywhere—but I never wanted to listen to it. I must have shut myself off from my memory of it for a reason. To protect myself. A defense mechanism. The human brain is clever like that.

I know that he stayed in the room for seven more minutes. I know that people were talking about logistics and legalities. I know that I was referred to as 'the legal wife.' And I don't really know much more.

Afterward, I cried into my mother's arms. She cried too. Annmarie was still here. She patted my back in a way that I think was supposed to be comforting, but was anything but. Her nails were too long and they kept catching on the woolen jumper I was wearing. A jumper I chose because it was the first one that Ruari had given me. Out of all the jumpers.

And he didn't remember me.

[Silence for five seconds]

Summer Taylor-Braddon: I began researching his condition a lot. Trying to work out if there was any way that his memory would come back. The doctors told me he'd been diagnosed with retrograde amnesia, and I began reading everything I could about it. It was a condition where memories from before a certain event were lost. Sometimes, these memories would just be inaccessible for a while, but other times, they'd have been deleted from the system, so to speak.

Ruari's memories hadn't returned in three years, and so his was considered permanent. But the more I read, the more I held out hope that it was just that he hadn't been in the right environment to remember. I was who he needed. I could unlock his past for him. I could save him.

I spoke to his doctors frequently—as his wife, they didn't question giving me information, though some of them seemed surprised when they saw me in person.

"I thought you had darker hair last time we spoke," one said—which didn't make sense at all and clearly meant they were getting mixed up with another patient's wife.

It turned out that Ruari had been in and out of hospital a lot in these seven years, and in recent weeks, he'd had a few overnight admissions too. He'd been unwell, suffering from headaches, and it was noted in his file of course that he'd had an accident three years ago and had lost all memory thereof from before.

And I was leaving the hospital, one day, when I.. This woman stopped me. She had her hand on my arm, and she was trembling.

"Are you okay?" I asked. I had assumed she was another patient waiting to see the neurologist.

But she didn't seem like she was. There was something about the way she was staring at me.

"Are you Summer?" she asked. "Summer Taylor-Braddon?"

"Who are you?" I asked the woman. She was skinny, leggy, and had gorgeous eyes. Her dark hair was long and sweeping over her shoulder.

"Mia," she said. "Robert's wife."

[*Silence for five seconds*]

Summer Taylor-Braddon: Okay, so at first, I didn't really take it in.

I stared at this beautiful woman, and I thought, *Okay, who the hell is Robert and why is this important?*

Mia was watching me closely, carefully. There was something about her dark eyes that was alluring—like I was iron filings being drawn to a magnet. She shifted her weight a little and her coat fell open. And I saw. I saw her belly.

She was five months pregnant. That was when it hit me.

Robert. Ruari.

"His wife?" I stared at her. "But… but…" I couldn't get the words out. They just got stuck. Stuck on my tongue, my tongue that suddenly seemed too big for my mouth—and it was still swelling, swelling like her belly, because I blinked and I suddenly saw it: Mia nine months pregnant, Mia giving birth, Mia presenting her baby to Ruari. His baby.

I let out a choking sound.

"I'm not supposed to talk to you," she said. Her voice was so, so soft. There were dark circles under her eyes. "But I just… I had to come." She tucked a loose strand of dark hair behind her ear. "We've been together years."

Her belly was all I could look at, and suddenly it was like I had x-ray vision too, not just glimpses of the future. Because I could see the child inside there. What it meant.

"I'm his wife." At last, I bit out the words. At last, I felt like I could finally say something. "We got married. We..." My face crumpled—I felt it like it happened in slow motion, all the muscles suddenly sagging then growing taut with tension, with despair.

I wanted Ruari back.

I wanted my life back, our life back.

And then Mia—this woman that I suddenly had so much hatred for—put her arms around me. She held me and I didn't want to be held by her. I didn't want to be against her belly—against their child—but she held me as I sobbed, and I was just too weak, too exhausted to move.

"We're not officially married, but we may as well be." Her tone was cool, and she pulled back from the embrace. Her hand found her bump, and she cradled it.

That should be me.

I gulped in air, too quickly, ended up with hiccups. "He's my husband." I held my hand up, showed her the ring. I'd never taken it off. Ever.

"I shouldn't be here," she said, and then as quickly as she'd arrived, as she'd sought me out, she left. Just like that.

I watched her leave. Her long coat flapped in the breeze.

He's with her. He's got a kid on the way.

[Silence five seconds]

Summer Taylor-Braddon: "It doesn't matter if he's lost his memory," my solicitor told me. "He's still legally married to you. And he cannot marry Mia Wilson, not without divorcing you first."

Divorce?

I choked.

"But for the time being, in the eyes of the law, you're his wife. He is currently undergoing psychiatric evaluations, and depending on the outcomes of those, decisions about his healthcare would come to you if he is not deemed of sound mind."

Marriage does not depend on recognition. I can't remember who told me those words. Whether it was that same solicitor. But they swirled round and round my head. Ruari losing his memory, having this whole other life for the last six years, didn't change a thing.

I had Ruari back, and I was going to be with him again. I was sure of it.

Now, we'll just take a look at the newspaper headlines from that week, and then we'll bring my guests in.

TAYLOR-BRADDON ADMITS SHE'S GOING TO KILL MIA WILSON

OUR FAVORITE WRITER HAS A NEW VICTIM IN HER SIGHTS

TAYLOR-BRADDON TO KILL HUSBAND'S LOVER

ARE WE ABOUT TO FINALLY GET A BODY IN THE SAGA OF SUMMER TAYLOR-BRADDON?

KILLER WRITER TO STRIKE AGAIN

SUMMER TAYLOR-BRADDON VS. MIA WILSON: THE CAT FIGHT WE ALL WANT

Adelaide James: I thought you weren't going to bring another journalist in.

Summer Taylor-Braddon: Dante is here in his capacity as my friend, not as a journalist. Now, I'm stepping out of the room for this first part—it will be easier. Adelaide, you may remain only if you are silent. Do you understand? Because Dante will kick you out of the studio if you don't follow the rules.

Adelaide James: You really are a piece of work, aren't you?

Summer Taylor-Braddon: Just be quiet. No speaking until I tell you, okay? I'll be back shortly. This next part of the story is going to be told in alternating segments between me and him. And I mean it, Adelaide—one word from you in this part, and you're off the project.

Dante Fiore: And now we get to the part in this incredible story where it makes most sense to talk to you, Robert. To find out what happened. Now, you've asked for us to call you Robert—as you said that's the only name you remember, and we will get to this of course, but I think, we just need to start from the beginning with you—the beginning of this incredible sequence of events. So, you're in Indonesia. What next?

Robert Hayden: [*He laughs, dryly*] I don't recall being in Indonesia at all. I… [*He sighs*] I was in water though. I remember that, the darkness of it, and the immense pressure—right here, inside my skull. And something hit me on the head. I've got this scar here. But I don't remember that actually happening. There's nothing really.

Dante Fiore: And yet you ended up in Australia?

Robert Hayden: Bigge Island.

Dante Fiore: So this is off the coast of Western Australia?

Robert Hayden: Yeah. Kimberly region.

Dante Fiore: And I must say it's remarkable that you actually have an Australian accent now.

Robert Hayden: [*He laughs*] The locals wouldn't agree with that. They assumed I was English. That's how I came to be known as Robert… but I feel like I am him, even now. I know what was apparently my own life way less than his… God, this is all so fucked up.

Dante Fiore: Sorry, I should just let you talk. So, tell us it all.

Robert Hayden: So the island is sort of owned by a group of Aboriginal Australians. I can't remember their group's name, sorry. My memory's awful, even now. But they found me. I… I was swept up on their shore. I was unconscious at that point, but they dragged me in. There was a broken wooden door or something near me and we think now that I'd been on that. That that's how I got across the ocean from Indonesia. Must've taken weeks. I don't know.

It's so bizarre thinking about it. I don't know how I survived.

But the locals thought I was this English photographer, Robert Hayden. That's how I became him—and I really thought I was him. They showed me a photo of him, and while I had swelling on my face and all these cuts on my neck and arms, I did look like him. I had no reason to doubt that I wasn't him.

I mean I couldn't remember otherwise.

The photographer had apparently been visiting Bigge Island on his own, as he was solo traveling for a couple of years. He'd only been missing for a day or two. And then the locals found me, and they knew that there was this man missing. And I looked like him.

The locals looked after me for a few weeks, I think, treated my injuries with their bush plants. But I couldn't remember a thing. There was a white man there as well, at one point—and he was the one who said I must be Robert. The locals had been calling me a different name up until then, but now I really believed I *was* Robert. I thought this newcomer had recognized me, and it was such a relief. It was like finding myself.

I didn't stay on Bigge Island for all that long though. When I got a bit stronger, I was back on the mainland, staying with a family that the Indigenous people on Bigge Island knew. One of them was a doctor, and he said I should go to the hospital for a CT scan or something.

So I did. We went there. But there was nothing. No problem.

I still couldn't remember who I was, but everyone was saying I was Robert. The missing photographer. I used to literally tell myself that. "I am Robert Hayden. I'm thirty-one years old." The doctors at the hospital said that my lack of memory was probably psychological. There was no physical reason for it. My brain scan was fine. And so that was that, really.

At some point, Robert's possessions were brought over to me. I had my passport, an English driver's license, bank cards, two rucksacks full of clothes, and a whole load of photography equipment that I had no idea how to use. I also didn't know the password for the phone, or the PINs for the bank cards. But I knew what all of them were, like I knew how Western society worked. It was just anything to do with who I was that I didn't know.

I stayed in contact with the people who'd found me, and with that family on the mainland too. They helped me loads, and one of them knew a tech guy. He got me into my phone and then I was able to go to the bank, get access again. I honestly hadn't thought that that would work. But it did.

I expected that I'd feel more like myself—like Robert—as time went on. Everyone seemed to think that I'd start to get my memories back, but there was always just this nothingness. It's so weird, when you can't remember who you are. It's like you start again, like learning to talk and learning to walk. Except you're a grown man and you can talk and walk—only you wonder who taught you.

I pictured my parents often—these imaginary faces, faces that would change and mold. I'd spend hours looking in the mirror, trying to work out which of my features might be transferable to their faces. Were my eyebrows like my father's? Did my mother and I share a nose?

It's so strange, because I never really concentrated on my own face, on how I looked—because I was a stranger. I didn't even recognize myself, that's the extent of my amnesia. There was no recognition at all—even when photos would be taken of me, I'd look at them after, and there'd be this moment where I'd search for myself in it, but there'd never be that click. That moment of 'Ah, that's me.' Instead, I'd work out where I was in the picture by a process of deduction.

Across the next six months, I moved around a bit. I had money in my accounts, and I thought I was a photographer, so that's what I did. I was proper shit at it though. Like, really bad. So that didn't last long. Instead, I ended up lodging with the Wilsons, a family that ran a surf school.

And that was how I met Mia. She's their daughter.

Her whole family were just so, so kind. So welcoming to me. I ditched the photography, and I thought I'd do manual labour, but I just kept getting these headaches. Waking up in cold sweats in the night, really struggling to sleep properly. I was so drained and I just had no energy.

I kept thinking about that doctor that had said it was all psychological, and I knew that something must've happened. I'd been found half-drowned or something. So, yeah. [*He laughs a little*]

The Wilsons had originally been giving me reduced board rates in exchange for manual labour, but Rick realized I couldn't do it all. He was kind though. He's this big guy in his sixties. Really strong, muscular. I was chatting to him one evening about it all, that I just still couldn't remember who I was. Of course he could see my scars on my face, but I showed him the ones on my sides too, and my back. "Something happened and I don't know what," I told him.

And he said something like, "Looks bad."

We were smoking a couple joints by that point—all the Wilsons did. Usually in the evenings, after they'd closed up the surf school. Their place was directly on the beach, and Mia and her sisters would be out having fun in the water. Wetsuits. Long blond hair, they all had, apart from Mia's. Hers was jet black. They all looked good, the Wilson sisters. Mia, Teyah, and Andi. So Mia's the oldest. Then there's Teyah—she's really loud. Like, always talking. Andi's quieter, more like Mia, I guess. But Mia's got more confidence.

All three were late twenties, only like a year or so between each of them, and they were all just so relaxed. So happy. Always laughing. Like, in the evenings, I'd just hear them and it would bring a smile to my face.

But yeah, back to that evening, Rick said they were looking for someone to do admin in the office. Taking bookings for their lessons. That kind of thing. He offered it to me, and I was just so grateful. The idea of just traveling around again with a few bags just really scared me. I felt so unanchored, even though every family I'd stayed with was so welcoming, treating me like one of their own.

So I began working at the surf school, and of course that meant that me and Mia got closer. She was a trained lifeguard too, I discovered. She'd done some qualifications in it down at Bondi, I think. She was proper respected now, though she later told me she'd had some wild days when she was younger—a time when she'd really gone off the rails. But we'd hang out quite a bit. Especially once I started doing the admin work. I'd be at the office quite late, and usually once she'd finished teaching the teenagers, she'd pop back into the office.

She started bringing me a cup of coffee, and I didn't have the heart to tell her I couldn't stand the taste of it. I just really liked talking to her. She'd still be in her wet suit, but she'd take the top half off, have it hanging around her waist. The wetsuit arms would fly about from her hips as she'd walk, and it was just mesmerizing. She'd have a bikini on underneath, of course, but I think it was pretty obvious that she knew I was interested in her.

How couldn't I be? Damp hair hanging about her shoulders, in beautiful waves. Sorry, you probably don't want to hear this, do you? You're Summer's friend.

Dante Fiore: I want to hear your story—whatever it is.

Robert Hayden: Okay, well, we got together. It was just fun at first, reassuring, warm—more and more, I realized that she was the person I just wanted to be spending more time with. Just being around her made me feel different, lighter. It made me forget that I had this past life I couldn't remember, that I didn't really know who I was, because when I was with Mia, we were making new memories, and although I was still struggling with forming new memories, there was always something of them that was left within me. I'd see her each day, recognize her, think fondly of the time we'd walked down on the beach together, or when we'd been listening to music in the office, or grabbing some food, and I'd feel this warmth. This reassurance. This sense of it just being right, you know?

Mia and I would hang out in the evenings at the pub too. I met all her friends. Sometimes her sisters would be there too, and she treated me like I was normal. That was the thing I really liked, really appreciated about her. How she saw me as Robert, not the man who can't remember or the man who nearly drowned or the man who washed up on Bigge Island. I was just *me*. And it was like she knew who I was, even if I didn't.

Mia's pretty health-focused. I mean, all the Wilsons are. They may go down to the pub, but they don't really drink all that much alcohol. Mia keeps track of what she drinks and eats, not to the extent that she's logging calories in an app or anything, but she's conscious of her body. Of what it needs.

I'd order the same each time we were at the pub—a couple of pints, which began to become three or four—and she'd still be there, drinking a lemonade or an orange juice. She never really judged me for my drinking—and I didn't really realize that I had a problem with it either, because drinking, well, it was the only time—other than when I was with Mia—that I could truly forget my problems. It felt familiar, a glass in my hand. A bottle clutched in my fingers. A crate of cans hugged to my chest. It felt right, and it made me wonder about who I was before. Just a little bit, among the haze.

Although I had access to my social media accounts—Robert Hayden's—they didn't go back all that far, and what posts there were, were pretty sparse. There were messages too, friends who'd check in. Friends who I didn't remember, no matter how many times I looked at their profiles or photos that included them and me.

"Think of it like a game," Mia said to me one evening. "Like piecing together the story." My phone was on the bar in front of us, and the pub was loud but not too loud. We could still hear each other, hear ourselves think.

And I replied to her something like, "What if I find out I'm a criminal?" and I laughed, even though I didn't really feel like laughing, and even though my life wasn't a game.

But Mia laughed too, and that's when she said it. She said, "I love you," and she was still laughing, her warm hand on my arm.

She loves me? I balked and I felt so sweaty all of a sudden. There was a bitter taste in my mouth from the beer I'd been drinking. Suddenly, I wanted to throw up.

But I didn't. I just looked at this gorgeous woman in front of me. My only true friend. My best friend.

We'd known each other six months, and I couldn't imagine moving away from her, not seeing her. Mia really was the light in my very dark life. And she loved me.

And so I told her that I loved her too.

We kissed then, the first time. Her lips tasted sugary. I held her gently, and I felt this thing building inside me. This urge to be with her, to never let her go. Of course, I expected to feel something down below too—

only I didn't, and that confused me. Because she was gorgeous, and I should've been feeling that.

I didn't tell her, of course. How could I? When I loved her.

We hung out together more and more. I all but moved into the Wilsons' family home, leaving the little annex untouched for days. And I realized how much I was relying on Mia.

I was still struggling to sleep, and I was getting these nightmares now too. Really bad ones. Of drowning, of being in water, in darkness. Of a woman shouting my name, but I could never actually hear what she was shouting. It was just this sound, but it stirred something in me. Something frightening.

I'd wake, crying, sometimes, and Mia would be there. Holding me. Telling me it was okay. We figured it was just from the near-drowning I'd had off the coast. She told me over and over that I was lucky to be alive. That I was meant to find her.

It was… We were intimate, after a few months—I think she was surprised how long I waited… but I… God, I can't believe I'm telling you this… I thought I should've liked it more. I just felt awkward… And I always felt like there was this wall between us. Not because of her, but me. This wall that I couldn't break down, couldn't get past. It was like I couldn't *feel* things properly. We'd have sex, and I really wanted to feel something—I was desperate to. But I didn't. I couldn't. But it wasn't like the sex was bad. That was the really confusing thing. It just didn't really do a lot for me.

I didn't look forward to it like I thought I should've.

Mia said that was okay—not that I really told her everything that was going through my head—and she said that it was the trauma I'd been through. She did research on it, read some of the stuff to me. It made sense, but I also wondered if maybe I was gay or something. Had my accident meant I'd completely ghosted a boyfriend I'd had or something?

When I was with Mia, even though I was absolutely in love with her, I still felt like I wasn't experiencing attraction in the right way, and this just really fueled my nightmares in a way that I didn't understand, couldn't understand. Because I'd hear this woman shouting what I was sure was my name—even though I couldn't hear what my name was—and then suddenly I'd be out of the water with all that crushing darkness, and I'd be in these castle ruins, and there'd be a man sitting on the ground in front of me. He had like a hammer and all sorts of tools, and he was digging and looking for stones or something, and I just didn't understand what any of it meant.

That dream kept happening, and I kept feeling so bad. Who was that man? And why wasn't I dreaming about Mia? I'd told her I loved her, and I really did. Because even though I didn't feel like I was attracted to her in the way I thought I should be, I was in love with her. I can't make that clear enough—because everything in my life felt so uncertain and new. Except Mia. She was my familiarity. My home. I wanted to spend all my time with her. I just… I had to be with her.

We had been together for three years, when Mia told me she was pregnant. I was surprised. Like, really. Because we weren't really sleeping together all that often. When we did, it was her that initiated it, and more often than not, I just did it because I felt that that was expected of me. That was my role.

But then the baby came along—and there was something about seeing Mia pregnant that just made us closer. My baby, growing inside her. Holding her, holding them both. I've never loved anyone more.

As time went on, I did start to feel more attracted to her as well, and that in itself was a relief, even though I still felt like I wasn't feeling it in the right way.

We were still living with the Wilsons when Alex was born, but when he was about a year old, we realized we needed our own space. Mia had quite a bit of money saved up, so we were able to rent a place for ourselves. I was still doing the admin work for her family's business, and it made sense to continue that— especially as I was the only one earning now. And I really felt like the Wilsons were my family. Really did. Rick and Yvette, they treated me like I was their son. Anything I needed, they were there for me.

About a year later, our second was born. A little girl. And I named her this time, because Mia had chosen Alex's name, and I… I named our little girl Summer. I never knew where the name came from, still don't know if it's a coincidence or not, but… but our girl's called Summer.

I think that was one of the things that Mia found hardest, when we all learned the truth. Looking at our girl and knowing that she's most likely named after Summer Taylor-Braddon. That a part of me remembered my past life. That I'm not actually Robert. It's all just such a mess.

But it wasn't for another two years until we found out who I was.

Mia was pregnant again. After Alex was born, you see, we'd decided to have a couple more, so we were trying. We got Summer quickly, and that almost made the sex easier for me, like I knew it had a purpose, a function. We'd get a happy baby at the end—and I discovered I loved being a dad. It's like I was made to be a dad.

It took longer, with our… our third. And Mia was five months pregnant, and little Summer, well, she wasn't well.

She'd been quite a sickly baby. In and out of hospital. But she'd just been diagnosed with a condition and it meant that me and Mia also had to get tested. There were so many tests, and I can't even remember at this point how it came out, but it turned out the real Robert Hayden had had some DNA tests done before. They were on the hospital system, so he must've had it done in Australia, before he went missing, before I inadvertently took over his life. And then something in my bloods showed a mismatch and—and I wasn't him. It was as quick as that. One click of the computer screen, a doctor looking at me with a confused face. And my whole life—the last six years that I'd been living as Robert Hayden—everything was just upended. Again.

Dante Fiore: That must've been quite a shock.

Robert Hayden: It was, because I'd become Robert. I'd really grabbed hold of that identity, made it my own, because I didn't have anything else. And it felt like this massive loss. Like something huge had been ripped away from me. Everything, taken. And I was left with what felt like nothing. Not knowing who I was again. Because although I'd never remembered my life as Robert, I was still him. I'd lived as him for six years.

I was engaged to Mia, and she was going to become Mia Hayden, and it was all just… such a mess.

Mia was confused and angry—she thought at first that I'd tricked her. But I hadn't. I hadn't tried to deceive anyone. She said she still loved me though, that we'd find out what had happened.

And of course, I was still part of her family. We had kids together. Another on the way. But she and I spent ages trying to find who I was. We figured I was English, because of my accent—even though I had now developed an Australian twang—and so we began looking and looking for any missing English men.

It felt ridiculous at first, and it also made me question why I'd not done this before. Why I'd just accepted I was Robert.

But Mia said to me, "You wouldn't question it though, would you? Someone gives you a passport, says it's yours, says your Robert Hayden but you've had an accident that's affected your memory, you're not going to question it."

And I said, "I suppose so."

But I still felt guilty—like deep inside I'd known, even though I hadn't.

It wasn't just guilt about that though. Guilt about the real Robert Hayden. Where was he? What had happened for that man to go missing? Was he dead?

Had me stepping into his shoes meant that no one would actually look for him? Could he have been saved?

To this day, we still don't know what happened to the real Robert. And that keeps me awake at night, often more than anything. I feel haunted… by him, maybe, I don't know. Haunted by something. Like I played a huge part in this crime against him. I stole his life, because I didn't have one of my own.

I tried talking about this to Mia soon after we learned that I couldn't be Robert, but she snapped at me. I mean, it's not fair to say that about her, like, she's been amazing. She was pregnant too, of course. And this was all a lot of stress and shock.

She just told me not to worry about who Robert Hayden was. To worry about who I was.

And then we read about Ruari Braddon.

[Silence for five seconds]

Robert Hayden: It was weird—because I knew immediately that I probably was him. Ruari Braddon. Not that I felt a connection to the name or that any of my memory came back. It didn't. There was still nothing.

But there were photos online. So many photos. And they looked like me. More so than any of Robert's had, even though we'd thought Robert's photos did look like me, at the time.

Plus, there was also so much information about how Ruari had disappeared.

"On honeymoon in Lombok," I remember saying to Mia, "disappeared during the tsunami."

And I remembered it—the crushing weight of the water. How dark it was. The pain in my lungs. And a woman. A woman calling my name.

But that was all I remembered.

We went to the police, me and Mia. And that just started it all off… this whole, well, it felt like an explosion. There were DNA tests done, and police from the UK and also Indonesia were involved. The DNA tests confirmed it. I was Ruari Braddon.

That was such a weird hour—finding out for sure. I felt like it was something to celebrate. Getting my life back. And yet I couldn't celebrate it. Mia couldn't either, because we read online that Ruari Braddon had been in Indonesia with his new wife, and we'd seen photos of her. Summer. It was such a gut-wrench seeing her name. It made Mia physically sick.

I looked at photos of her, my *wife*—photos of the two of us that had been published—but I didn't recognize her. Or remember them being taken, those photos. But I wondered if I'd know her voice, when I heard it. If she was the woman in my nightmares who'd been calling my name for years.

It was such a weird feeling. A yearning, almost. I both wanted it to be her voice, and not. And of course, I was scared. Scared what all of this meant.

I said to Mia, "I'm still with you," one day, because I could see she was worried. I think it was a couple days after the DNA confirmation. She was scared.

Doctors got involved too. Suddenly, everyone wanted to be doing tests on me, scans. And I mean *everyone*. I had to undergo psychiatric evaluation too.

And then I heard that my *wife* was flying over. This Summer Taylor-Braddon who I didn't know. But maybe I did? And it was all so confusing.

I… I think a lot of people thought I did remember Summer though, at least partly, because I'd named mine and Mia's daughter after her—that's what they said. Rick got particularly mad at me one day about it. But he calmed down. Mia made him calm down. She held my hand and told me—and everyone—that we'd sort this. We'd work things out.

But I felt like a fraud. A criminal. Like I'd done something wrong. I couldn't shake that feeling—and it's still with me now. It's like being haunted, and there's absolutely nothing I can do about it. It's torture, it really is.

And I've got my little girl—Summer Hayden, that's her name. But I'm not a Hayden. The real Robert

Hayden is still officially missing, and I thought about him too much of the time, back then. Well I still do now, but then? Then it was driving me mad. And my little girl, I kept fixating on that, that she should be Summer Braddon, only that's just messed up, because my wife and… I had a wife I didn't remember, and a girlfriend who I was scared was going to leave me. This whole thing was just… It was a lot, you know.

And of course my daughter wasn't well. I'm not going to disclose her medical details here, because that's private. But Mia and I were spending so long at that hospital, only now there were British consulates getting involved. All sorts of other people too—reporters, journalists. The press were everywhere, camping at the hospital. And I just wanted to be with my girlfriend and daughter. Little Summer was undergoing treatments, and I needed to be there for her—only I couldn't. Because all of this was happening, and Mia was getting fed up with how she couldn't drive to the hospital with our daughter without paparazzi following her car.

But we were being followed, all the time. It was so stressful. People were shouting at me, shoving microphones into my face. Yelling at me. Constantly there were camera flashes. Cameras were even directed into our house. Someone got a photo of Mia as she got out the shower one day. It was all over the papers.

And it was getting worse.

The constant hounding of the media.

I hadn't really expected it, but the day when I was going to meet the woman who was apparently my wife I had to have security with me. Apparently, this had been a massive case in the UK. And Summer—this wife I didn't remember—was famous. Like, proper famous. We'd seen she'd written books, but we hadn't quite understood just how big a deal she was. Or how a big deal all of this would be.

I was so nervous going into the hotel, to meet her. I was told her mother was there too. A woman called Margaret Taylor. Apparently, Summer and I had lived with her when we were younger. Before we got married. And Margaret had even taken me in when I'd had some problems at home.

My heart was hammering so fast as the door to Summer's hotel room was opened. I can't even remember who else was present. I just looked at this woman, at Summer Taylor-Braddon, my wife—and I didn't remember a thing.

Summer Taylor-Braddon: I hated Mia from then on. The new wife. The other woman. It didn't matter that I didn't know her at all, that she'd shown me that bit of kindness. She was public enemy number one. She had taken Ruari from me.

Now, of course, I can think a bit more clearly. Not objectively, mind, because I'll never be able to think objectively about any of this. But I know it wasn't fair to her, all that happened. She had no idea that her Robert was missing British national Ruari Braddon. She was just in love.

Oh and she was pregnant, of course.

Again. They already had two kids. One of which ironically shared my name. As if this situation couldn't get more messy.

When I first heard the daughter's name, it had given me hope. That maybe, even though Ruari hadn't appeared to recognize me, there was still a part of him that could remember. That the memories weren't lost.

But it didn't seem to work that way. There was still just nothing in his eyes, when I saw him again too. At the hospital—because he was having more tests done. Every doctor in Australia suddenly wanted to be the one who'd treat him, unlock all his memories. It was as if they just needed to find the right key, but the problem was there never was a key that was the right fit for his mind.

Or if there was, that key was at the bottom of the ocean.

Whereas Ruari was speaking with a damn Australian accent of all things, really believing he was this other person. A boyfriend. A father.

I think maybe that was the part I found the hardest, about Mia. That she was living what should've been my life, with my man. My kids.

She had everything I'd ever wanted.

I watched Mia from my hotel window, one day. I'm not really sure why she was back, down there. But she was. And suddenly, her swelling belly just seemed so massive and I felt sick looking at it, imagining Ruari's kid inside there, incubating, like this was some high-tech sci-fi show.

My breaths suddenly got too loud and then I threw up—no warning. Just watching, through streaming eyes, as my vomit laced the windowsill and those stupid frilly lace curtains.

Mia was talking to someone down below outside. There were police down there and other official looking people. She also had a couple people with her that I assume were friends—and that, that really got to me. Made me want to cry and scream.

Dante Fiore: Why's that?

Summer Taylor-Braddon: I haven't really got any friends now.

Dante Fiore: You've got me, Hana, Ash.

Summer Taylor-Braddon: Yeah, I have. But I was meaning my *girl* friends before—Hana and Julia. I haven't really got them. I mean, Hana *is* still my friend, you're right. But I don't know if we're as close now. And then there's Julia… I don't think she and I can ever be friends again. Not properly.

Dante Fiore: You're not alone though.

Summer Taylor-Braddon: No. I've got my mum, of course. I wouldn't have survived all this without her. But I do miss Hana. I miss how things used to be.

Dante Fiore: Have you tried reaching out to them?

Summer Taylor-Braddon: No, and I don't know if I can. It feels like that ship has sailed. This whole life that I have—it's sailed away. I had finally got my husband back, only he was no longer Ruari Braddon. He was a stranger.

[Silence for five seconds]

Summer Taylor-Braddon: The media really made my life hell—even more so—after Ruari was found. Of course, they found out about Mia, I think they actually knew about her before I did, and they spun this whole angle about how I was trying to break up their love story.

The papers just wanted me to be the villain. Like, they really hated me. They made it out like I'd been abusive to Ruari. That he'd finally done what he had to, to escape me. It's ridiculous, but that's what they said.

And they loved Mia. Of course they did. She was the innocent bystander in all of this, and her only crime was that she loved the man that I was set on destroying—that's literally what they said.

They pitted me against her constantly. She was the angel, the princess. I was the witch, the devil. And they really loved that—there were some cartoons going around, about us. I'm sure you saw them?

Dante Fiore: Yes, I have. It's shocking what they did to you.

Summer Taylor-Braddon: Of course, there were still people who were still loyal to me—I saw their comments on Facebook posts, defending me—but their voices were just swamped. There was this huge tide of anger, and it was directed at me.

Mum and I were pretty much having to move about a lot. Different hotels in Australia, as they kept finding out where we lived. I didn't really mind the constant check-outs and check-ins though, because I was just so set on getting Rauri back. On him getting better. On him remembering me. And it seemed to me, that if I had to just put up with all this media hate on me, to get him back, if that was the price I had to pay, then I could do that.

Because Ruari, getting lost in the tsunami, swept all those miles, and not knowing who he was? Well, he'd been through much worse.

Ruari Braddon: I guess it makes sense now to call me Ruari from this point on, right? Now we've got to the point where we know who I am?

Dante Fiore: Whatever you feel more comfortable with.

Ruari Braddon: [*He laughs, dryly*] I don't know if I'll ever know who I am.

Dante Fiore: Would you like another cup of coffee?

Ruari Braddon: No, thank you. The only drink that could calm me right now would be something with, like, 90% alcohol, and I better not. That wouldn't be a good thing for either of us. [*He groans*] God, this is all so messed up, isn't it? Even just thinking back to it.

I was a mess, right after I'd had this reunion with the wife I didn't remember. It was hard on me, of course—and I knew it was hard on her too. I could see the desperation in her eyes, when we were in that hotel room. She wanted that moment of recognition. But I couldn't give it to her.

But most of all, it was hardest for Mia. She was… She had a conversation with Summer. She told me that, once we'd got back from the hospital the next day with JoJo—that was what we were calling our daughter now. Josephine was her middle name, and Mia just started using it. Then it became JoJo. But Mia was… she was really struggling. Like, massively.

She asked me, "Are you going to leave me?"

And it didn't matter how often I told her I wasn't, because she was my life now, because she always seemed to think that I'd go back to Summer. She was so, so scared. And I often felt that I couldn't comfort her either. I couldn't give her the support after everything she'd given me—my whole new life. And I'd just ripped hers to shreds.

Summer Taylor-Braddon: Ruari's father flew out at some point. I'm not too sure when, but suddenly he was just there. It was the first time I'd actually met him, as he'd not come to the wedding, and though I'd been on video calls with him—all those times when Ruari and I sat in our flat, awkwardly talking to Maverick, I wasn't prepared for just how different this man would be in person.

For one, Maverick was six foot five. This was something that Ruari had never mentioned to me before, and with Ruari himself being five foot eight, I'd never even considered that his father might be very tall.

Maverick wasn't just tall though. He was built like a tank. His voice that had come across on our Skype calls as strong and rich was actually booming and very, very loud in person. He made quite the dramatic entrance, in the hotel lobby. Mum and I were sitting there, waiting to meet with a woman called Vera. I'm not too sure what her job title was, but she was acting as a counsellor really, helping us all navigate this tricky situation. And so Mum and I weren't really talking, but rather anxiously waiting when Maverick Manners strode into the hotel, wearing these ginormous shoes that seemed comically big.

I recognized him instantly—and he saw me, but he didn't even stop to say anything. We made eye contact, and then he strode right on past me.

That was all I saw of Maverick, that day.

You want to know the thing that upset me the most?

Ruari remembered him. And I didn't even find out at the time. It was a week later, when I was speaking to Ruari's doctors.

Ruari Braddon: It was weird, when my dad came. This huge ape of a man. Apparently, I rarely even saw him before. He'd been in and out of prison.

But I saw him. And there was just a part of me that knew who he was—instantly.

"Dad," I said.

And he looked shocked that I knew him, but then he said something like, "Ah, they told you I was coming." Because of course he'd been told I had no memory.

But I said, "No."

And we had this moment, this really weird moment, and my head began to hurt a lot. Because it was coming back.

Dad—living at his house—talking about Mum and Al—and…

And I remembered Mum and Al.

And Dad. Most of all Dad.

But I looked into his face, and I thought of how when I was Robert, looking into the mirror, trying to put together images of what I thought my parents might look like.

And now, here he was. My dad.

And I knew him.

And I remembered him.

And oh dear God. Fuck. I remember that thinking those words—because I then realized it. I might remember my wife too. And if that happened, I just didn't know what it would mean for me and Mia.

Summer Taylor-Braddon: "It is very promising that Ruari recognized his father," the doctor said to me.

The chair I was sitting on felt too cold, too hard, and its seat was too long. Its sharp edge pressed into the backs of my legs, just below my knees, and I'd been shuffling about a lot, trying to get comfy. But the doctor's words froze me. I couldn't speak at all. I mean, I tried to, but my throat was too thick, and I just couldn't make a sound.

"It leads us to believe," the doctor continued, "that the rest of his memory may come back. He may remember you too, in due course."

They said it was like it was a wonderful prospect—and it should've been, of course. Only I couldn't help thinking that it would just make this whole mess even worse. And then I hated myself for thinking that, as I'd do anything to get Ruari back, and if he remembered anyone, it should've been me, not his deadbeat dad.

I don't recall what else was said—all I can remember is how I pressed my legs into the sharp edge of the seat then, because it was painful and I wanted to concentrate on that, the physical pain, rather than the gaping hole inside me. Why would Ruari remember his father and not me?

"It just doesn't make sense," I told Mum later. "It really doesn't—that man wasn't there for him at all! Not when it mattered."

"Oh, love." Mum hugged me, and I breathed in her perfume—that thick… *clagginess*. It wrapped around me like it was suffocating me.

Like I'd never breathe again.

[She clears her throat] Ruari's father got him to move back to England though. To move in with him. Mia and the kids too. It was January this year—2024—when they finally did it. Just like that, they were back on my home territory.

Not the same town, of course not. Not even the same county. They were living in Bristol.

I stayed firmly in Okehampton, but I had these dreams of getting the train up to Bristol, of storming around there. Of making him remember me—doing whatever was necessary to ensure. Because Ruari, my Ruari, he was still in there. I just had to find a way to wake him up.

I kind of became fixated on that. I was spending pretty much all my time, trying to find a cure for his amnesia. I mean, I had his phone number and Mia's too, but I wasn't actually in contact with him any more. The two of them didn't want to be. But I still felt this urge to research, to find a way to bring Ruari back.

Mum said to me more than once that it wasn't healthy, that maybe I should just let him go. He had a new life, after all. Kids.

But he was *my* life.

I read about hypnosis, psychotherapy, all these different things that could apparently bring memories back. I wanted to find out if he'd even come back to Okehampton at all, if he'd walked the places that he used to be familiar with, if anything had prompted his memories, but I just couldn't bring myself to text him. I think I was scared that he'd tell me he had but that the answer was 'no'. That that part of his life was maybe just gone. That it wasn't there, waiting to be recovered.

Ruari Braddon: We did go back to Okehampton, me and Mia. Well, it was mainly me that wanted to go. She didn't. She was pretty stressed. She was thirty-four weeks pregnant by then, and we were living in Bristol. Pretty near the city center. I thought she would've liked it there. Liked the arts culture. The music.

But she was missing the surf life. Missing Australia really.

We kept having arguments. I kept telling her it wasn't good for the baby.

She kept telling me that none of this was good for her.

I was sure she was going to leave me. Several times, I even wondered if that was best. If maybe I should never have been with her, because apparently me and Summer Taylor-Braddon had an amazing love story. I read her book, you know. *The Saga of Me and Him*. I felt the characters' love for each other. And I read all these interviews that Summer had done, where she said she'd been writing our love story, what we should've had.

I felt sick after reading them, the interviews—and also that first book in her series.

But I also felt... I don't know. This sense of excitement. Of freedom.

I found myself Googling Summer a lot. I'd have little JoJo on my lap, bouncing her on my knee, and I'd be scrolling through Summer's website. I'd be searching for her on Facebook, trying to make sense of my life.

Of course, she wasn't on social media anymore.

I read a lot of the posts people were making about her. The names they were calling her.

Her life seemed like a living hell.

And yet, mine and Mia's, ours was heading that way too.

I don't know what really made me decide to go to Okehampton. But I knew one morning that I had to.

It wasn't just that I wanted to find Summer. I wanted to find myself.

Mia wasn't happy when I told her. Not happy at all. But she said she was coming with me. Maybe she was scared I'd see Summer and remember being in love with her. Or maybe she was scared because Summer was still my legal wife.

I'd spoken to a few lawyers about the legal stuff. And although Mia had been pushing me to get a divorce from Summer, I hadn't made any of the official steps to doing so yet. I guess a part of me thought that it wouldn't just be a divorce from Summer. It would be a divorce from who I was. Who I am.

We traveled down to Okehampton on a Sunday. A couple of hours in the car. We left Alex and JoJo with my dad. I'm still not sure that was a good idea—an ex-con and all that—but that's what we did. And really, he did seem to be a good grandad. Better than he had been a dad, anyway.

It was raining when we arrived in Okehampton. Mia parked in Simmons Park. She was exhausted, but I hadn't been cleared by the DVLA for driving in this country. Not since I'd declared my amnesia. And it wasn't like it was something I could hide.

I found it weird though. I knew all the rules of the road, and I knew that I had learned to drive on the streets of Okehampton and the wider area, yet I couldn't remember those lessons. Couldn't remember the places.

Mia and I walked around for a bit. I think it was one of the first times when we'd had no reporters tailing us. No one following us. No one taking photos.

It felt like freedom.

And I didn't recognize anything in Okehampton.

We stood looking up the driveway at the school. Okehampton Community College. There are photos of me in their uniform—a uniform that had changed a few times since I'd left, so all the kids we saw milling outside weren't wearing that uniform that I'd worn— but I just didn't have any ounce of recognition.

Mia was tired, grumpy.

I was getting annoyed.

We hadn't told anyone we were coming here, and I wondered if that was a bad idea. If maybe I wasn't giving myself as much of a chance as I should've, as I deserved. I knew the names of my friends I'd had here—friends who still lived here. I mean, you, Dante, but also Ashley Kincade. Julia Rivers and Hana Burton. And Summer Taylor-Braddon.

Of course, I knew Summer's face. But not any of the others.

I wondered if I'd just walk right past them, if maybe they wouldn't recognize me either. I had changed a lot. Not just seven years older, but the scars on my face had distorted my features.

Still, I assumed they would've recognized me, had they seen me. My photos were all over the papers, the news, social media platforms.

They would've said something. They'd been wanting to see me. Ashley, especially.

But I didn't see anyone I knew. And no one seemed to see me.

I just felt like a ghost, wandering that town.

All in all, it was a bad idea.

Summer Taylor-Braddon: I told myself I just needed to move on. Ruari, though living in Bristol, showed no desire to meet with me. He had Mia. He had moved on.

Everyone was telling me to do the same.

It wasn't the ending of the love story that I'd envisioned, that I'd dreamed of, begged for.

But I needed closure. I really needed it, and so that's why I went there. Why I went to Bristol.

You all know that, though.

Everyone knows that—don't they? Because when I went to Bristol, to see Ruari, to try and work out what we were going to do, because just pretending that none of this was happening, well it wasn't working. But he wasn't there. He'd gone out with his dad and Alex. And hours after I arrived, Mia was dead at my feet, and everyone thought I'd done it.

EMERGENCY CALL AUDIO RECORDING

Emergency Call Handler: 999, which service do you require?

Summer Taylor-Braddon: Ambulance.

Emergency Call Handler: Connecting you.

Ambulance Call Handler: Ambulance Emergency, what's the address of the emergency?

Summer Taylor-Braddon: [address redacted]

Ambulance Call Handler: Thank you. And is the patient breathing?

Summer Taylor-Braddon: Yes, she is.

Ambulance Call Handler: Is she conscious?

Summer Taylor-Braddon: No.

Ambulance Call Handler: Thank you, and what's your name?

Summer Taylor-Braddon: Summer.

Ambulance Call Handler: Okay, Summer, tell us what's happening.

Summer Taylor-Braddon: I… I'm with a woman, and she's been stabbed in the stomach.

Ambulance Call Handler: Is the attacker still on the scene?

Summer Taylor-Braddon: No. We're inside now. She was stabbed outside, but I dragged her in here, into the house. I don't know if I should've moved her. But she's bleeding a lot, and I don't know what to do.

[Shouts outside can be heard]

Ambulance Call Handler: Hello, Summer? Are you safe?

Summer Taylor-Braddon: I'm safe. She's bleeding a lot.

Ambulance Call Handler: Paramedics are on their way, but I need you to get a clean towel or cloth. Can you do that?

Summer Taylor-Braddon: Yes. I can… Uh, yeah, there's a blanket here. It looks clean—it's not my house so I'm not sure… But I think… Oh God.

[A loud hammering sound follows, followed by more shouts from a male]

Ambulance Call Handler: What's happening, Summer? Hello?

Can you tell me what's happening?

Summer Taylor-Braddon: They're still outside, but… She's… She's been sick, and she's still unconscious. Should I put her on her side? Oh fuck—she's having a seizure. I don't know what to do. And—and she's pregnant! I forgot to say she's pregnant!

Ambulance Call Handler: Just stay calm please and listen. I'm going to tell you exactly what to do.

Summer Taylor-Braddon: I still just feel weird, hearing that call. Like it wasn't me.

Dante Fiore: But it was.

Adelaide James: Wait—is that an unedited recording?

Dante Fiore: It is. But please refrain from interrupting, Ms. James. Now, Summer, would you like to tell us what happened?

Summer Taylor-Braddon: Yeah. I would. Because even though the police cleared me of any involvement, there are still so many people out there who think I did this. The joys of being a crime writer, eh?

Dante Fiore: But this project that we're doing is to get the truth across. Your truth.

Summer Taylor-Braddon: It's not just *my* truth. It's *the* truth.

Dante Fiore: Sorry. Yes.

Summer Taylor-Braddon: So, I was kidnapped once. I bet you didn't expect me to tell you that?

Dante Fiore: Uh, no, I didn't expect you to say that—not now, anyway.

Summer Taylor-Braddon: I feel it's important for everyone to have this context. You included, Adelaide. Especially before we continue with the events of that day.

Dante Fiore: So, Kidnapped? What—I mean, how? When?

Summer Taylor-Braddon: I was five years old. I don't really remember it. Well, I might but I'm not sure. You know when you're little and you know something happened because you've been told it happened, and you sort of think you remember but the memory is mainly a construction, because you know?

Dante Fiore: Yeah, I think so.

Summer Taylor-Braddon: It's like that. Mum told me about it when I was ten years old. It was because I'd been having these nightmares where a long hand reached out of a white van as I was walking past, and the hand would grab me. Pinch me really hard.

I'd wake up crying and everything. And after the third time it happened, Mum told me about it.

Dante Fiore: What happened?

Summer Taylor-Braddon: It wasn't a white van or anything. It was at the shopping center. In London. We were there visiting Mum's cousin's nephew or something. I don't know. Me and Mum and Matilda. And Mum said Matilda really wanted to go in this shopping center, but everything was so expensive and so Mum didn't want her going in there because she'd feel guilt-tripped into buying something when Mattie found something that she absolutely adored and had to have. You know?

Dante Fiore: Yes.

Summer Taylor-Braddon: Well, it was when Mum and Mattie were arguing about it. Mum said we had to go back to the hotel, and Mattie was proper screaming about it. Fifteen-year-old girl having a sulk. That kind of thing. And Mum looked back down at where I'd been standing, and I wasn't there. She'd only let go of my hand for a few seconds. But that had been enough.

Dante Fiore: Shit.

Summer Taylor-Braddon: Yeah, shit. I mean, I kind of remember a man with kind eyes. I mean, I think I do. Might just be filling it in. But Mum called the police and the security of the shopping center all came out, the whole place was in lockdown.

And I was found in Pizza Express, of all places. Just down the road. With a man and a woman. They were in their forties, that's what Mum said.

And they told her they'd found me wandering on my own and so had decided to buy me a pizza. They told the staff at Pizza Express it was my birthday, and everyone in there was singing to me when the police came into the establishment.

Dante Fiore: Had you wandered off?

Summer Taylor-Braddon: No. I hadn't. They got CCTV later that showed the couple had been standing behind Mum when Mattie was getting all upset about not being able to go shopping. They'd, like, crouched down behind me, and I guess said something to me. I'd turned around, and they'd held their hand out.

It looked like I'd just gone with them willingly. Held their hands, and they walked me away. Bought me pizza.

Mum told me that they'd said afterward in interviews that they couldn't have kids. That they just wanted to know what it feels like. And this—this was something that I began thinking about a lot, as mine and Ruari's wedding grew closer. We'd decided to have kids, and I kept thinking, what if it doesn't work? What if the IVF fails?

What if we don't get a baby? Will my desire to have a child warp me and make me take some other person's kid? I mean, it's ironic now, isn't it?

Dante Fiore: I think everyone wonders if they have capabilities to do bad things. It's human nature to wonder. To think about what might push you.

Summer Taylor-Braddon: I had been desperate to have a baby with Ruari. So desperate. But I always told myself that I'd never just take someone else's child. I knew that was wrong.

Is it okay to just take a quick break now?

Dante Fiore: Sure.

Summer Taylor-Braddon: So, you know that I've not got the best mental health, right? I'd say that's probably been quite obvious. No, I'm not expecting you to answer, Dante. I'm just saying. Not that it's an excuse for what happened—but I didn't actually do anything. I didn't act on those thoughts.

And everyone has these thoughts, right? The majority of us just ignore them. I mean, I've spoken to my therapist about them—they're intrusive thoughts. People get them all the time. Everyone does.

And I did ignore them. Those thoughts.

So, uh, back to what happened, then, I guess.

Well, I'd already learned by this time that the two kids were called Alex and Summer, of course. Did I already say this? I can't remember. But, anyway, I… I felt that the girl's name had to be a sign. I'd had that dream again, where I was pregnant with Ruari's baby, only this time, when I was giving birth, Mia was the midwife.

And she was so angry at me.

She shouted that I had stolen him from her, and then suddenly, she had hold of my baby. A little boy. And she was running away with him, screaming that it was her baby.

I knew I had to get my baby back. I was desperate to. Like, I had no choice. That was my baby she was taking, and my motherly instinct or whatever it was kicking in. I was still in my hospital gown, and like the placenta or umbilical cord—whatever it is—was hanging out of me, and I was running after her, down this corridor with these tiny fluorescent lights.

And all I could concentrate on was getting my baby back.

I woke, pretty panicked. I might've been screaming, because my mum was opening my door, all concerned, asking if I was okay. And I had this huge ache in my arms. Like, something was missing. My baby.

You have to understand that I hadn't been sleeping at all. How could I? I'd had more death threats, and some journalists had got hold of my new phone number—did I tell you I'd had to change it so many times? And I was just having to have my phone turned off pretty much all the time, but I was always anxious I was missing calls. Important calls. Like from the lawyers, solicitors, police.

I still had my laptop on though—like, all the time. I don't know why I did it, but I'd set up Google alerts for my name and Ruari's name. And Mia's too. And I was, like, addicted to reading all the toxic things people were writing about me. It was horrific. And it made me feel so much worse, but I just couldn't stop. My eyes would be so blurry and I'd be exhausted, scrolling through page after page of hideous comments about me. Calling me all sorts of names. But doing that was better than sleeping—lying there, trying to get to sleep in the dark room, because that's when the reality of it all would come crashing down. That Ruari was no longer mine. That he'd never been mine again. He was hers. My thoughts would just feel like knives. They'd stab, stab, stab me. I wouldn't be able to breathe. It was that bad—it would keep me awake. It was like torture. Thinking of them, together.

I kept imagining them in bed. They'd obviously slept together, whereas Ruari and I never had. It made me wonder if he was no longer ace, if that was even possible. If maybe he'd just pretended he was to try and reassure me. If he'd been giving up sex the whole time we were together.

She could give him what I couldn't, and I really, really hated her for it. I felt so threatened by it, all those nights when all I could do was think about her and him and *them*, but at times, I also didn't hate her—like at the same time as hating her, and it was just so, so confusing. So, I was confused. I was sleep-deprived. Like, seriously. I couldn't function. I was losing weight.

Mum got me some sleeping pills. Just over-the-counter ones. I didn't want to take them because I didn't want to be trapped in nightmares. Nightmares, where I was convinced I'd see them together. Maybe kissing, or actually doing it. And I didn't want that.

But Mum persuaded me otherwise. She said you didn't dream if you slept because you'd taken pills. That the medication interfered with something in your brain, stopped your dreams, nightmares.

I was reluctant, but I agreed. I was desperate.

And so that's when I took them. That's when I slept, finally.

And that's when I had that dream—me, having Ruari's baby, and Mia taking it away from me. Stealing it.

When I woke up, I was disorientated. Very disorientated.

But I was thinking that the baby she was pregnant with was actually *my* baby, and somehow just knowing that their daughter had my name confirmed it—even though this was about the unborn baby, not Summer. I know it sounds ridiculous now. I know that.

I didn't make the journey up there, to Bristol, straight away though.

I walked around like there was cotton wool in my head, for days. No, cotton wool's not right—something warmer, fuzzier. You know that feeling when you skid on carpet, and it's like a friction burn but not quite painful? But warm? Yeah, well I felt like that, on my skin. Only it was the inside of my skin. Like, everywhere.

I wanted to turn myself inside out, so I could scratch myself raw.

I wanted to bleed and feel something, let it all out. Just stop it all.

But I couldn't.

And I… well, I wasn't well. Really wasn't well. No one could be, not in my situation.

I didn't know what to do, other than to take more sleeping pills, because I thought that would mean I'd be back in that dream, where Mia was running away with my baby, and I could chase after her there. If we were in the same place. If I just dreamed again.

But when I took the sleeping pills the next night, I didn't dream. There was nothing. I woke feeling numb.

I remember looking at the TV the next morning. There was some program on but there was a pregnant woman in it. I saw that as a sign. It was almost like the character was saying 'Go and see Mia. Get your baby back.'

I deserved a baby. I deserved just a bit of their happiness. Because it wasn't fair that Mia had taken Ruari from me.

And I guess, well, I also wanted to see Ruari again. So that's what I did. I went to Bristol. I'd had their address for a while. It was written in the back of my notebook.

I didn't go on my own though. Ashley came. It was weird, how that worked out. So, I don't know if we've covered this—I can't remember—but as soon as Ruari had been found, Ashley was, like, in contact with me all the time. Wanting updates. When I was back in Devon, he was suddenly round at my mum's house every day. And James too sometimes. I mean, Hana was as well. And Julia—this was before she did the bad thing.

Ashley had gone to see Ruari once, but he didn't remember him either. But Ash arrived at mine just as I was trying to find Mum's car keys. [*Summer laughs*] I mean, I couldn't even drive so I don't know why I thought that I was going to literally drive to Bristol. To Ruari and Mia's.

I guess I was a bit frantic, because Ashley was asking if I was okay. And I said something like, "I'm going to see Ruari."

And then he thought that maybe if we *both* went, it might prompt something. I think he said something like "Just immerse him in his old life and he has to remember, right?"

So, Ashley was driving me up there. He had this gray Polo. And I was feeling really… well, not great. My head was pounding. We had a couple hours, because the traffic was bad. There'd been snow and ice, and some accidents. Ashley suggested I got some sleep. Said it would be better if I was refreshed when I got there. I guess I must've looked really awful.

I had my pack of sleeping pills in my pocket. I remember being surprised, finding them there. But I took them—maybe too many, I don't know. I don't think I was being careful, but there I was, napping in his car, and I had this dream where I found Mia. She was in a hospital. Pretty similar to the one where Ruari had had more tests done, where I spoke to his doctors and found out that he'd recognized his dad.

Mia had these really long arms in my dream though, and I realized at one point that I was suddenly holding a baby—the baby—but she wouldn't let go. No matter how far I ran, she would still be holding onto the baby. Her arms would just elongate, stretch. A bit like that *Doctor Who* episode with David Tennant and Catherine Tate. You know the one, right?

Well, anyway, after that I just kind of woke up in a bit of a state. And I just had this voice in my head saying that I had to take the baby. Like, that dream just really cemented it for me, and I'm not sure why, when I guess the dream was kind of saying that Mia would never let one of her kids go. But at the time, in the back of Ashley's Polo, where the heating was on too high, and I was stretched out on his back seats but had really bad cramp in my right leg, I just felt like I'd be restoring things to their natural order, if I took her baby. Making things right again.

Of course, I *didn't* do that. I mean, for one, Mia was still pregnant with her third child. I don't know how far along she actually was but to me, she looked like she must have been due any day. But even if she wasn't pregnant, I'd never have actually done anything about this. I'm just being upfront about this all because everyone found out about my crazy nightmares and thoughts later. But I did not do anything to harm Mia or any of the children. I just want to make that clear now. It was only a thought—just for a moment. I wasn't ever going to act on it.

But I did go up to Bristol.

Dante Fiore: And now we've got Ashley Kincade coming into the studio. Hello, mate. You're right on time. And just to confirm, Summer is still here.

Summer Taylor-Braddon: Yes, hello. [*She pauses*] I don't know why I felt the need to say that. I've just been talking for, like, ages.

Dante Fiore: Adelaide James is also still here, too, though she's purely a listener for this part.

So, Summer and Ash, go ahead, you guys. Whenever you're ready.

[Silence for five seconds]

Summer Taylor-Braddon: Well, we'd better get started.

Ashley Kincade: It was almost dark when we arrived in Bristol. Ruari's address was only about twenty minutes from the train station. Temple Meads, that is.

Summer Taylor-Braddon: And I was awake by then. Properly awake. And though I'd had those thoughts, those dreams, I knew I wasn't actually going to do anything. In fact, I didn't really know what I was doing up there.

Ashley Kincade: You said to me that we should go back.

Summer Taylor-Braddon: And you said that we could if that's what I really wanted but that it seemed a shame when we'd just driven through the worst traffic ever to get there.

We didn't go back though. We just got to the address—or rather, the road. Their house was at the end of a cul-de-sac, but there was nowhere to park down there, so we'd turned around.

Ashley Kincade: There were cars everywhere, parked. And I ended up driving back, quite a way, before we realized that I'd just have to drop you off.

Summer Taylor-Braddon: So, you dropped me off.

Ashley Kincade: Well, actually, I really cocked things up first, didn't I?

[Silence for three seconds]

Summer Taylor-Braddon: I wouldn't use that phrase, but, well…

Ashley Kincade: God, I can't even believe I did that. Like, still. But yeah. Just before Summer got out the car, well… I made a pass at you, didn't I?

Summer Taylor-Braddon: You… you decided that then was the best time to tell me you'd been in love with me all this time.

Ashley Kincade: *[He laughs]* I am still just so embarrassed by it all. But yeah, I'd been so nervous the whole way up to Bristol. And I was just thinking that you and him were going to get back together. That you'd… just fall in love again, and I'd have to watch you two be together all over again.

But I thought if I told you first, then it might change things. Change the pattern in the cosmos or whatever it is. That maybe you'd realize that Ruari could be with

Mia and then you'd be with me. That there'd be a person for everyone.

Summer Taylor-Braddon: I can't remember what I said.

Ashley Kincade: You said, "Uh, okay." And then you got out the car, and you walked away.

Like, I'm still really sorry about that.

Summer Taylor-Braddon: It's okay. So, yeah, you were going off to find somewhere to park, and then you were going to meet me at Ruari and Mia's house. It was really cold too. It wasn't snowing, but there had been snow. It had sort of turned to this gray slush at the sides of the pavement, but everywhere felt really slippery. I had to walk really carefully. And… well, as I walked, I realized someone was following me.

A woman. She was pretty small. Petite build. Immediately, I was just so annoyed. And so fed up. I wanted to scream at her. I assumed she was a reporter. A journalist. That she was going to hurl abuse at me.

But she didn't. She didn't say anything, until I was a few hundred yards from the address I had for Ruari and Mia.

And then she came right up to me, and I got a little worried. But my head was also hazy still, so I didn't really register what she was saying to me at first.

But she was saying, "I'll sort this for you." Saying it over and over again.

Under a street light, I got a good look at her face. She was blond. Kind of beautiful, really. And she had these really earnest eyes. And she was still saying to me, "I'll sort this for you."

I sort of shook her off. I don't know if I actually said anything back to her, but then she was just gone. Just like that. Vanished.

I began to wonder if I'd imagined it. If there'd been no one around at all. Like, I wouldn't have been surprised if I'd been hallucinating.

There was a big icy patch outside the garden gate for number 11. That was their house. A frozen puddle, I think. And I tried to step around it, while reaching to open the gate, but I ended up sort of slipping on it anyway. I had Crocs on. Mum's Crocs. I don't know why. But I grabbed the gate to steady myself, and there was a sharp bit on the gate. It cut my hand.

Anyway, I was halfway down the path through the little garden when the front door opened. And I was sure that that was going to be it: the moment that I'd dreamed of. Where Ruari would look at me and he'd remember.

He'd remember everything.

But he didn't.

Because it wasn't.

It wasn't him.

It was Mia.

She looked tired. That was the first thing I saw, and I don't know how I saw her face so clearly when my vision was still a bit blurry. I had this pain in the back of my eyes, but the pain felt a bit like a comforting blanket by then. Reassurance.

She looked at me and her mouth dropped open. She said, "What are you doing?"

And I said, "Hello," and then I didn't know what to say. She looked about ready to drop—and I remember thinking how even though she was so obviously tired, she had this glow to her.

And then I was about to ask whether Ruari was in, when… It all happened so quickly.

There was just this blur of movement—like, really quick. And that woman—the blond one from a few moments earlier—she was here. I didn't realize she was holding a knife at first. It was only when she was right in front of Mia, and when Mia made this strange noise, and then when Mia sort of fell in slow motion, reaching out to the doorframe, trying to catch herself on that—her fingers, just stretching out, but missing anything, grasping at empty air…

Mia fell, and the blond woman turned back to me, and she said, "I told you I'd sort it."

Ashley Kincade: I heard the screams.

Summer Taylor-Braddon: It was me screaming. Mia didn't make a sound. She just…
She didn't make a sound.

Ashley Kincade: It was… Man, I don't know.

Summer Taylor-Braddon: I had never seen that woman in my life before that day. I didn't know who she was, or anything.
She just ran off.
And I was left with Mia, bleeding at my feet.
Of course, I tried to help her. And I had my phone in my pocket, so I was calling an ambulance. Had to wait for it to turn on though, because it was off. It was off in my pocket.
And I kept looking around. I thought the woman was still nearby. I could hear other shouts now—some sounded like her, but there were men's voices too. I was so scared.

[Silence for six seconds]

Summer Taylor-Braddon: I called the ambulance.

Dante Fiore: And you'd already got Mia into the house then, hadn't you?

Summer Taylor-Braddon: Yes. I don't remember doing that, but I guess I did. I told the ambulance person on the phone that we were inside.

Ashley Kincade: When I arrived, you were scared to let me in at first—you thought it was someone else, didn't you?

Summer Taylor-Braddon: I was so scared.

Ashley Kincade: But you let me in. Mia was still breathing, but it was erratic. And she was unconscious. I took over. On the phone to the emergency services, but also doing CPR. You'd started it by then, hadn't you?

Summer Taylor-Braddon: I… I was so scared.

Dante Fiore: Are you okay, Summer?

Summer Taylor-Braddon: Yes. Sorry. Thank you.

Ashley Kincade: People were congregating outside, before the ambulance arrived. Neighbors, mainly. I think, anyway. But we didn't open the door until it was the paramedics shouting.

Summer Taylor-Braddon: I… I think I knew then, that Mia was going to die. I… I felt so helpless.

Dante Fiore: I can't imagine how traumatic it must have been for you.

Summer Taylor-Braddon: I'm glad Ruari wasn't there. That he didn't see.

But she wasn't alone. When she…

Her breaths got all raspy. Right before the paramedics did arrive.

I held her hand.

She whispered my name, and she pointed up. At the ceiling.

Ashley Kincade: The paramedics arrived then. I let them in. They needed space, to work on Mia. They asked though if anyone else was in the house.

Summer Taylor-Braddon: That's when I realized. Their daughter. She was upstairs.

I went upstairs. Sat with her. Made sure she didn't come down.

Summer must've been two or three. I… She kept speaking, asking me where her mama was.

I'd thought the first time I met Ruari's kids would be magical.

Instead it was… It was that. Then.

It was… [*She clears her throat*] There are no words for it, you know?

Ashley Kincade: Mia was pronounced dead at the scene. We didn't know where Ruari was then, but there was concern. The police arrived. They were trying to locate him.

Summer Taylor-Braddon: Of course, people thought I'd done it. It didn't matter that the Ring doorbell footage proved otherwise. People thought it was me—like, even weeks after the police had cleared me, there were so many people online who said it was me. Yet another trial by media.

That one was bad, too.

Really bad.

And they… they found out about my nightmares. About how I'd had these thoughts of taking back 'my' baby—those thoughts that I only had for a brief time. It was shortly after this all happened, that I just mentioned to a few people about them.

Ashely Kincade: We were at your house. Me and Dante, Hana and Julia. You.

Summer Taylor-Braddon: I just mentioned it in an offhand way.

Ashley Kincade: We'd opened a couple bottles of wine. We were… We were trying to decompress, I guess. And I was talking about the nightmares I'd had since. And you started talking about all the nightmares you'd had, since this whole thing started.

Summer Taylor-Braddon: And then a couple days later, suddenly the press all knew about my nightmares. No guesses, eh, who wrote that first new article?

Apparently 'a source close to me' had told Adelaide James. And then she said I'd been planning to abduct Mia's children and cut the unborn baby out of her once she was dead.

I was pissed off. Only four people knew about my nightmare, and I asked them all—but each of them assured me they'd not said a word. I believed them. I really did. I didn't think they'd betray me. So, I assumed that the room had been bugged again. Like at the hotel in Australia.

Bricks were thrown at our windows. There was this rag soaked with petrol pushed through our letter box.

Mum and I were moved into witness protection. We're currently still there. Well, we're in the process of getting new identities. But of course for this project, I'm using my old name. The name I can never use again.

Not even for writing. I don't know which name I'll publish under next, but that's not the point.

SUMMER TAYLOR-BRADDON'S SICK MURDER PLAN

By Adelaide James

It's the stuff of nightmares and horror films. A woman, heavily pregnant, is killed and her unborn baby is cut from her womb. The person doing this unspeakable act? A scorned woman, a childless mother, a psychopath. Or, in this case: a bestselling writer.

So, we all know the story with Summer Taylor-Braddon. How she persuaded her husband to hide away for years so they could pretend he was missing. But how, when he eventually resurfaced, Taylor-Braddon found he'd gone off-script. He'd only gone and got himself a girlfriend and become a father.

It's only understandable, that Ruari Braddon would do that. For the years when he and Taylor-Braddon were together, she'd locked him into a sexless relationship. And men have needs!

Now, Ms. Taylor-Braddon found herself with a script that other people were writing. She had to make her characters do what she wanted again—and I guess she wanted the baby.

Ms. Taylor-Braddon's plan didn't quite work however. Because while she murdered Mia Wilson—her husband's new woman and the true love of his life—the unborn baby also died.

What I find shocking though is how Ms. Taylor-Braddon hasn't been arrested on two counts of murder.

She's still out there, and shouldn't that scare everyone?

Ashley Kincade: The woman who killed Mia—she was detained. Caught. She's serving life now.

Summer Taylor-Braddon: But it's not over for me. It's never over.

I blink, and I see her dying in front of me.

Ruari's lost, again. He's…

He doesn't want to see us again. He moved somewhere else. But I don't know where.

He did speak to me once, though, on the phone. We were finalizing our divorce. [*She gulps*] He thanked me for trying to save her.

As if I'd do anything other than try to save her.

I'm not the monster people think I am.

Ashley Kincade: They only think that because of Julia. No one close to you actually believes that.

Dante Fiore: What happened with Julia, Summer?

Summer Taylor-Braddon: It was her. She was the 'source close to me'. All that time. She was the one giving so much information about me to the press. She was…

Ashley Kincade: She said these people offered her a lot of money.

Summer Taylor-Braddon: She sold me out. My so-called best friend. I mean, she's tried to apologize since. But there's no way back from that.

Day Four
Wednesday July 24th, 2024

Adelaide James: Okay, so I must admit, you told us quite the tale yesterday, Ms. Taylor-Braddon. And I do believe that that audio played of the emergency call has been doctored—I researched your friend Ashley Kincade last night, and didn't he do a course in media studies? I am sure he has the skills for editing audio, if you do not. Because I emphatically *do not believe* that you actually tried to help Mia Wilson.

Or if you did, it was to cover up your own actions. Make people believe you were helping when you weren't.

Summer Taylor-Braddon: You're speaking quite fast now, Adelaide, like you're… unsettled. Or unsure. Was yesterday the first time you heard that call?

Adelaide James: It was. But, as I said, I do not believe that what was played was the original recording. And now it's time to actually give readers the truth. Because isn't that what this whole project is about? The truth.

Summer Taylor-Braddon: It is, yes.

Adelaide James: Well, I'm not going to beat about the bush here. I've got my final guest waiting outside. I'll just invite her in now.

[*Sounds of the door opening and closing, amid a third person entering the room*]

Adelaide James: Let's welcome Mary Smallridge. Say hello to her, Ms. Taylor-Braddon.

Summer Taylor-Braddon: Hello, Mary.

Adelaide James: It's been quite a while since the two of you met, has it not? Well, I'll get straight to the point. Mary was best friends with Ms. Taylor-Braddon's sister when the two were at Okehampton College. It's got to be about twenty years since the two of you left, right?

Mary Smallridge: Yes.

Adelaide James: I must admit, Mary, I was very intrigued when you got in touch with me. You gave a wonderful interview back then, but I was never entirely sure what I wanted to do with it. I wrote up articles, but my blog just didn't seem like the right platform for that. What you told me felt too big.

But when Ms. Taylor-Braddon invited me onto this project, well, I couldn't believe it. All my dreams just came true—just like that! So, Mary, if you'd like to tell the tape recorder what you told me before, that would be wonderful.

Mary Smallridge: I'd rather not speak in front of Summer.

Adelaide James: Would you leave, Ms. Taylor-Braddon?

Summer Taylor-Braddon: No, I will not. And this is my project, and you cannot force me out of this. Mary, go ahead though. I'm certainly intrigued about what you could possibly say.

Mary Smallridge: It's about your sister. Matilda. We were friends.

Summer Taylor-Braddon: I know that.

Mary Smallridge: We were sixteen, I think. When… when it happened.

Adelaide James: When *what* happened, Ms. Smallridge?

Mary Smallridge: When Matilda told me that Summer was the most important person in her life. And that she'd do anything to protect her.

[*She gulps*] We were… we were a little drunk at the time. In my bedroom. "This Love" by Maroon 5 was playing really loudly. My parents were out. Me and Matilda, we were lying on my bed, and we'd been talking a lot and she just blurted all this out—how she'd do anything to protect her sister.

And I said to her, I asked her, "Like what?"

And Matilda just said, "Like murder. I'll kill anyone who ruins my sister's life."

Adelaide James: Thank you, Ms. Smallridge. That's all we need to know. Would you like to leave the studio now?

Mary Smallridge: Yes, I would.

[*Sounds of Mary Smallridge leaving*]

Adelaide James: So, Ms. Taylor-Braddon, let's talk about this. You and your sister, and your sister's apparent ease of planning murder.

Summer Taylor-Braddon: That wasn't what Mary just said.

Adelaide James: You personally described the woman that you saw stab Mia Wilson as blonde. Yet in all the photos, the woman who was detained and convicted was brunette. But your sister is blond, is she not?

Summer Taylor-Braddon: If you're suggesting that Mattie had anything to do with Mia's death, you're completely wrong. That is just ludicrous.

Adelaide James: Only I have been trying to find your sister, and Matilda Taylor is proving a little allusive to find. Which is strange, given that she's normally very much in the public eye. What with her job and all that. All those tasteless photographs.

Yet, she hasn't updated her social media since the day before Mia Wilson was killed, has she? And she hasn't taken on any new modeling jobs—in fact, her agency told me she's left. No one seems to be able to contact her, so where is she, Ms. Taylor-Braddon?

Summer Taylor-Braddon: If you're suggesting that my sister did this—just… wow.

Adelaide James: I'm suggesting more than that. I'm suggesting that you were also involved. What was it that you yourself report the murderer as saying? Were the words, "I told you I'd sort it?"

Summer Taylor-Braddon: My sister did not kill Mia. We know who did. The woman is in prison.

Adelaide James: Well, if Matilda Taylor has nothing to do with this, why has she pretty much disappeared? She's untraceable right now. One might say she's *missing*—now, isn't that a familiar storyline?

Only you don't seem overly concerned—or indeed, concerned at all—this time? You're quite calm, which leads me to think that you're in on it.

Summer Taylor-Braddon: You are grasping at straws here, Adelaide. That's all you've got. And you're wrong.

Adelaide James: Then tell me where your sister is.

Summer Taylor-Braddon: She's traveling. And for her own safety, I am not going to disclose any more details. I know what you're like. I know what you're capable of. And I also know what readers are capable of—not just yours, but mine too.

The police concluded that the woman who murdered Mia was one of my fans. She thought she was helping me.

Adelaide James: Or it was your sister—your sister who was helping you. Helping you get your life back. Only it still hasn't gone to plan, has it? You haven't got your husband back.

Summer Taylor-Braddon: You can spout whatever lies you want, Adelaide. But I have told the truth. I have only ever told the truth. And when people listen to this project, they'll know. They'll know what I have been through. And they'll also see how toxic you are.

Adelaide James: I think people will make up their own mind about you, Ms. Taylor-Braddon—master liar and manipulator and murderer. Because you may have asked your sister to kill your rival, but the blood? Well, that's on your hands.

Summer Taylor-Braddon: We're never going to agree. But thank you for doing this project with me, Adelaide. It's been insightful. And thank you for showing your true colors. I think we'll stop here.

Dante Fiore: Okay, so this is our final few minutes recording this project. In this studio, I am joined by the two main people themselves: Summer Taylor-Braddon and Ruari Braddon. Now, I understand that this is the first time you two have been together, in the same room, since the tragic events?

Summer Taylor-Braddon: Yes. That's correct.

Ruari Braddon: When we were recording here yesterday, we sort of ended up avoiding each other. Even though we were alternating sessions. I think you were in the café, waiting there, so you wouldn't see me?

Summer Taylor-Braddon: Yeah, I was. I just… That waiting room outside this studio, it's pretty small. I know that if I sat there with you, Ruari, I'd feel forced to make small talk. And that didn't feel right. It's… It hurts being this close to you. And knowing… knowing everything that's happened.

Ruari Braddon: I still don't really know how this has all happened. How… [*He chokes up*] It's been six months since Mia was killed. Murdered. On our own doorstep. Because of all of this mess.

Summer Taylor-Braddon: I do feel horribly guilty that it was one of my fans who killed her. That that woman said she was doing it for me. I never wanted that. Ever.

Ruari Braddon: I know.

Dante Fiore: So, my question now is, what's next, for the both of you?

Summer Taylor-Braddon: Mum, Matilda, and I are getting new identities. Mum's going to start dialysis very soon. She's getting a kidney transplant. Anonymous donor. I would've—but I wasn't a match. Neither was Mattie.

We're moving. Quite far away. And I guess it will be good to have a fresh start. It's the only way, I think, we can move on. Away from everything.

This project, this is the last you'll ever hear of Summer Taylor-Braddon. She will no longer exist, as soon as this tape stops recording.

Ruari Braddon: I don't think I'm ever going to move on. [*He clears his throat*] I listened to the recordings, you know. This project. And it's… it's so difficult for me, because I still haven't got my memories back, but I'm looking at you now, Summer, and I feel this sense of… familiarity. Of knowing you.

And I'm so grateful that you've asked me to review all the tapes, to check that I'm happy with those being released. It makes sense that I'm asexual—that's the only thing that has made sense to me, in this project.

And I'm fine with that being out there, because we need more people talking about it, don't we?

Asexuality is real. It is a thing. It's not made up. Men, women, and nonbinary individuals can be—and are—asexual.

But I can't remember you, Summer. I can't remember any of the things you spoke about. Our time together. All I remember is Mia. And Mia's gone. And our baby. It was another girl, the third one.

But they're up there. Mia and the baby. They're looking over me, and I'm going to continue on. I have no choice. I've got Alex and JoJo to think about. I lost the love of my life—twice—but they're still babies themselves, and they've lost their mother.

They're not going to lose me.

It hurts, of course it does, seeing them. Being with them every day. It can't not. JoJo's really starting to look like her mum. But I… I have to be there for them.

And we're going to move back to Australia. They need family around. I need family around. The Wilsons… and everyone there who helped me, who looked after me. They're the only family I remember. And it doesn't matter that I'm not related to them by blood, because it's what's in here—in my heart—that really matters.

It'll be better for the kids, to go back.

Those two—they're my forever, now.

EPILOGUE

I take a deep breath and lean back in the deck chair. The sand is warm beneath my feet, and I fix my gaze on the waves lapping a few hundred yards ahead.

It's a quiet beach.

Very quiet. Only a few people are about at this time in the morning.

But I like coming here. It helps me think. Helps me process and understand.

It's strange, producing a project, knowing it's the last thing that you—as that person—is going to do. Even though 'Summer Taylor-Braddon' will no longer exist tomorrow, I still want people to think well of her. It's important to me, more important than I can truly say.

She's me. My past.

And no one will know me, going forward.

I'll finally be anonymous.

Yet, I don't want her—my ghost—to be thought of badly. That wouldn't be right. I don't want to be constantly worrying. So, Summer Taylor-Braddon was a good person.

She was.

Even if my sister wasn't.

A seagull swoops down onto the sand a little way away from me. Its beady eyes watch me.

I don't know why Matilda killed Mia.

Or where my sister even is right now. I told everyone she was getting a new identity—and maybe she is. Maybe she already has a new identity, living out there, as someone else.

There's only one thing I know right now: The whole Taylor family will no longer exist.

With a sigh, I stand. The seagull flies away.

I think that's for the best.

ACKNOWLEDGMENTS

This was one of those books that I have wanted to write for a while. The idea came to me one evening, when I was doodling in my notebook, and suddenly, I knew I just had to write it. Unfortunately, at that time, I was under deadline for two other manuscripts that I write under my other writing name (Madeline Dyer), and I knew I wouldn't have time for this one for quite a while. I shelved the idea, and I hoped I would still feel as enthusiastic when I returned to it. That's always a risk for me, but this time, it worked. I couldn't write this book quickly enough.

The first draft just flowed out, and it really felt like the book was writing itself. I don't think I've ever written something so fast.

A huge thank you must go to my dad (a fellow writer and an amazing artist!) who workshopped the plot with me and gave stellar advice. He was the first person I told about this idea I'd had, and he helped me sort out (quite) a few of the problems I had with it (remember that time we stayed up until half-past-midnight, workshopping solutions, and then we were both really tired the next day!)

To my mum: I know that you're going to be the first person to finish reading this book when it releases (you always are!), and I want to thank you for your unwavering support.

To my brother: thank you for your support, your Geographical knowledge and the first-hand insight into various places you've traveled to.

To Sarah Anderson: thank you also for your beautiful design work on the cover and the interior pages of this book.

To Kielie Gorman, my beta-reader: thank you for your feedback, your wonderful suggestions, and of course for your enthusiasm for this story. Thank you also for your guidance on how emergency call handlers work and for reworking that script with me. Any mistakes are mine.

To Madelaine Couch: thank you for your meticulous eye for detail when editing this story.

To my agent, Amy Collins: thank you for supporting me, not just with my traditionally published novels, but my indie books too.

To my family and friends: as always, thank you for your support.

And to Michael, my dear husband: I know you probably won't read this book or indeed the acknowledgements (or maybe you will!) but thank you for always being there for me and for helping me be a writer.

ABOUT THE AUTHOR

Elin Annalise graduated from Exeter University in 2016, where she studied English Literature and watched the baby rabbits play on the lawns when she should've been taking notes on Milton and Homer. She followed this up by gaining an MFA in Creative Writing from Kingston University while she was also breeding Shetland ponies. Now she is pursuing a PhD at the University of Bristol, but she keeps finding herself distracted by her cute guinea pigs. Oh, and she keeps binge-watching *Call the Midwife*.

She's a big fan of koi carp, cats, and dreaming.

Forever Is Now is Elin's fourth novel, but she also writes darker fiction as Madeline Dyer.

ALSO BY ELIN ANNALISE

In My Dreams

My Heart to Find

It's Always Been You